THE MODEEN TRANSFORMATION

FRANK H JORDAN

ACKNOWLEDGMENTS

The situations, organisations, and characters in this book are fictional, and any resemblance to an existing or past entity is entirely coincidental.

This book is written in Australian English.

DEDICATION

*To Mum and Dad, thanks for your support and for always
being there.
And to my mate, Wayne, the original Salty Dick.*

THE AUTHOR

A long time fan of Lee Child's Jack Reacher novels and Matthew Reilly's fast-paced stories, ex-Army Reservist and Queensland author Frank H Jordan penned his own high-action series inspired by the brave men and women of the Australian Defence Force.

Enter, ex-SASR soldier Jo Modeen.

Modeen Transformation is the second book in the thrilling **Jo Modeen** series, and follows on from the book that started it all, *The Modeen Factor*.
And there are plenty more adventures to come....

Connect with Frank online at *www.frankhjordanauthor. blogspot.com.au*

THE MISSION

Things just got personal for NatSec agent Jo Modeen

Australian security agencies are on high alert in the lead-up to the 2014 international G20 Summit, scrutinising recent activity on the summit website and tightening security measures for the attending diplomats.
Despite this intensified vigilance even NatSec Intel can't know what the terrorist group 'The Spear of Allah' is planning, something ex-Special Forces soldier and now national security operative Josephine Modeen is about to discover in a very personal way.
And for her there's more than national security at stake....

Josephine Dakota Modeen, recipient of the Medal of Gallantry and the first woman to be accepted into Australia's elite SASR, found life after the Army unfulfilling and her job as a security guard, boring. While wondering if her disapproving father had been right about military service being a 'poor' choice of professions offering few post-service career options, she was unexpectedly contacted by her old CO, Victoria Cross recipient Ben Logan, now team leader with covert Australian security agency NatSec.

She knew it wasn't a social call. Hearing from Ben meant a mission, no exceptions. When, after confirming she still had the right stuff, he offered her a place on his team, her answer was a decisive, 'You bet.'

She couldn't anticipate the ripple effect that career decision would have in the lives of the people closest to her....

CHAPTER ONE

The sweeping driveways of Brisbane's inner city carpark crisscrossed as they spilled out onto Elizabeth Street adjacent to the Hilton Hotel's entrance.

On the fourth floor of the carpark, a federal officer prepared the ministerial high security 7-series BMW. Assigned to chauffeur the US and UK deputy secretaries for foreign affairs, the officer was busy going through routine security procedures. After checking under the bonnet, he walked to the rear of the vehicle and opened the boot. Pulling out a long metal handle fitted with a mirror on one end, he extended it to its full length and used it to check beneath the limousine for any foreign objects.

The fresh-faced young officer was ambitious and wanted to impress his superiors. He'd accepted the 'babysitting' assignment gladly, thinking this would at least prove his alacrity if nothing else. Newly trained, he knew his mop of sandy hair, freckled nose and ready smile had some veteran officers eyeing him dubiously. If he were to prove his worth to his sceptical colleagues and ex-Fed father, he had to start somewhere. And being minder to some high-profile VIPs was an opportunity to prove his competence for more important tasks.

After completing a full circuit of the car, he went to the rear of the vehicle and opened the boot again. Retracting the mirror, he leaned forward to place it inside the compartment, only to have it slip from his fingers when his hand jerked into a rigid claw. As his body slumped head-first into the boot, a pair of strong, dark-skinned arms swiftly folded the officer's lower body in behind him.

Removing the silencer from his nine millimetre Glock and returning the gun to its shoulder holster, Nasir Aldin took the young man's standard Fed issue sunglasses off his now flaccid face and reefed the suit jacket from his lifeless body. Dark blood oozed thickly from the back of the officer's head as Aldin donned the dead man's jacket, closed the boot, and jumped into the limousine's driver seat.

Abdul Azeez sat on a lounge in a quiet corner of the Hilton Hotel's lobby. Dressed in a charcoal grey business suit, he kept his gaze focused on his smart phone, only lifting his eyes to scrutinise passers-by.

A portly statesman stepped out of the lift, accompanied by a tall, equally distinguished-looking man. They strolled purposefully through the luxurious foyer toward the sliding glass doors leading outside, onto Elizabeth Street. Seeing them, Azeez stiffened and gripped his phone tighter. After sending off a quick text, he shifted uneasily in his seat.

Throwing the concierge a brisk nod as he passed the counter, the portly statesman caught sight of someone sitting in a plush armchair in the brightly-lit lounge area. He pulled up short and called, 'I say, Modeen!'

Magistrate John Modeen immediately set aside the newspaper he'd been reading and rose to his feet. At the other man's approach, he extended a hand and smiled. 'Good morning, Sir Robert.'

Sir Robert shook his hand vigorously while also clapping him on the shoulder. 'Morning, old chap,' he said in a heavy British accent. 'How's the head, hmm?'

John rubbed his temples ruefully. 'Not too bad, thanks for asking.'

'Capital, capital! Glad to see all that excellent Scotch you imbibed last evening hasn't laid you low.' Sir Robert winked. 'What a charming function that was. First the Mayor and now the Premier, making us feel *quite* the VIPs. Oh, and in deference to Aussie informality, I insist you call me Bob. After all the merriment of last night's soirée, you, me, and Mike here,' and he indicated the tall man who'd strolled over to join them, 'should definitely be on first name terms.' His lips twitched and he puffed out his chest. 'I don't know about you Aussies and Yanks ...,' and he tugged at his jacket's lapels, '... but we English don't stand on ceremony.'

Mike guffawed and said with an American twang, 'Why, everyone knows that ... Sir *Barb!*'

'Oh jolly good!' Sir Robert chuckled. 'I love the way you Yanks mangle the Queen's English.' He turned to look up at John again. 'I *say*, old boy, I didn't realise what a tall fellow you are. *Quite* the "tall, tanned Aussie", aren't we?'

John gave him a smiling nod.

Sir Robert flicked the American a glance. 'Yes ... well ... one supposes you *colonists,*' and he grinned, 'had to grow large in order to salute the mother country from afar.'

'Shute,' Mike drawled with an amused shake of his head, 'I aint goin' down *that* road again. Got me nowhere last night 'n I doubt today'd be any different.'

The three men laughed as a white limousine with an Australian flag in the centre of its grille rolled up the circular drive and came to a smooth stop outside the doors. The driver stared forward with a blank expression, waiting patiently for his passengers.

'Ah, here's our conveyance. Good, good.' Sir Robert made to move toward the doors, only to stop and frown at John. 'I say, old chap, are you waiting for a taxi?'

'Well, I was about to have reception order one for—'

'Nonsense! You are most welcome to travel with us. I assume you are going somewhere in the city?'

'Yes, to the Magistrate's Court in George Street.'

'Jolly good, jolly good. Right, that's settled then. As you see,' and Sir Robert indicated the waiting limousine with a sweep of a suit-coated arm, 'we have plenty of room.' He smiled widely.

John dipped his head at them and bent to collect a brown leather attaché case from beside his armchair.

While they'd been talking, Abdul Azeez had skulked past and was standing by the limousine. On their approach, he bowed and opened the door, gesturing for the three gentlemen to enter.

Saying, 'I'll jump in the front,' John skirted around the back of the vehicle.

With an offhand nod at the man holding the door open for them, Mike got into the back seat and was settling himself when Sir Robert gave a grunt and fell against him. Mike felt himself pushed to the far side of the seat as Azeez jumped in beside Sir Robert, closing the door behind him with a thud.

'I say, old man, there's no need to be so rough,' Sir Robert said with a peeved frown. 'And it's a bit crowded in here don't you th—' He bit back the last words as Azeez made a show of pulling out a snub-nose thirty-eight special and pushing it deep into his portly side.

There was a solid metallic clunk as all four doors centrally locked. In the front seat, John Modeen's eyes widened as he gazed with disbelief at the chauffeur beside him. The olive-skinned man stared poker-faced back at him. He held a Glock low across his body, the gun's muzzle pointed directly at John's chest.

Barking in a foreign accent, 'Keep quiet and no one will get hurt,' the driver put the limo into gear and pulled out of the Hilton's circular driveway. Taking care to drive smoothly and not attract attention, he nosed the BMW into the heavy one-way traffic on Elizabeth Street.

Suddenly galvanised into action, John thrust his attaché case in the distracted chauffeur's direction and tried desperately to get his door open.

In the back seat, Azeez lurched forward and punched John viciously in the back of the head with the muzzle of his weapon. With a grunt of pain, John slumped forward, clasping the base of his skull as blood issued from the laceration in the thin skin and seeped onto his white collar.

'Now look here!' an outraged Sir Robert blustered.

'Shut up, *dog,* or I will do the same to you!' Azeez turned and shoved the bloodied snout of his revolver into the side of Sir Robert's flushed cheek, forcing his face sideways and back until his lips parted into a frightened grimace.

'Settle down! You must remain calm, if you want to live,' the driver yelled over the commotion.

With a final sharp flick of the gun's muzzle against Sir Robert's face, Azeez lowered the weapon but kept it trained on the two men in the back seat.

An uneasy silence, broken only by the rasp of harsh breathing, descended inside the limo as it made its way through the congested city streets and then out to the relative calm of the suburbs. Still rubbing the back of his head, John squinted out the window at a passing suburb name.

Eagle Farm.

The three captives sat stiff and silent as the limo weaved its way onto the back streets and then to a narrow, unsealed road. When they approached an abandoned shed at the back of an industrial area, Aldin slowed and then stopped the limo in front of the shed.

'Watch him,' he growled to Azeez, indicating John with a lift of his dark-stubbled chin.

Azeez grunted and tapped the back of John's seat with his gun as Aldin got out to open the shed's double doors. Returning to the vehicle, he nosed it inside the large, cobwebbed space, and parked it beside a late model white Ford Transit van.

Azeez immediately exited the vehicle and unlocked the van, opening the rear doors. Returning to stand at the front of the limo with arms extended, he aimed his thirty-eight special into the car.

'Get out. Slowly.' Aldin waved his pistol at the prisoners.

Gingerly opening their doors, the three men got out

of the car and stood on the filthy dirt floor. Azeez kept his gun trained on them as Aldin came around the back of the limousine.

He gestured toward the van with his gun. 'In there you will find grey overalls and baseball caps. You will strip to your underwear and put them on. Leave everything else on the ground.'

With a lift of his chin, Mike asked, 'Aren't you going to tell us what this is all about?'

Aldin merely raised his pistol threateningly and moved closer. 'Do as I say. NOW!'

Mike raised both hands defensively as, wincing, the three prisoners backed toward the van and complied. While they got changed, Azeez and Aldin took turns donning overalls themselves. When everyone was dressed, Azeez frisked each of the hostages and then ordered them into the back of the van.

From the pile of clothing on the floor he collected their wallets and pocketed them. After crushing their mobile phones under the heel of his boot, he bundled everything in his arms and dumped the pile in a dark corner of the shed. When Azeez had joined the three captives in the back of the van, Aldin locked them in, opened the shed doors, and then climbed into the driver's seat.

After exiting the shed and closing the doors behind them, he drove sedately to the Gateway Motorway and then deviated onto the Houghton Highway, before heading to Scarborough boat harbour.

Feeling the van come to a stop some time later, Azeez briefed the hostages, his tone low and guttural. 'You follow us to *ze* boat. You run, you die. You talk, you die. Understand?' He pointed the gun at each of them in turn as the back doors of the van were flung open.

Aldin stood on the wharf with one hand inside the lapel of his overalls. The butt of his Glock was just visible. With his other hand he gestured for them to get out the van. When Sir Robert hesitated, Azeez grabbed him by the scruff of his overalls and pushed him toward the doorway. Glancing at each other, Mike and John slid forward silently with Azeez close behind.

Once out of the van Azeez tucked his pistol under his overalls, keeping a firm grip on the weapon, and the four of them fell in behind Aldin. Throwing his prisoners a menacing glance, Aldin indicated for them to follow as he led them down a gangway toward a fifty-one foot Bluewater trawler. The nondescript boat sat serenely on the water, its battered steel hull an unremarkable deep blue. A colony of well-fed seagulls perched on its rigging. The birds watched as the five men boarded the trawler.

Azeez followed close behind the three prisoners and ushered them into the front hold, slamming the door behind them and turning the lock.

They stood in shocked silence for a moment, and then Sir Robert gave a deep sigh and said, 'Well I must say, chaps, I didn't see that coming.'

Running his eyes over the cramped hold, Mike dragged a hand over his short crop of grey hair. 'So … what the hell do we do now?'

John moved to stand beside one of the bunks. Sinking onto the cracked vinyl, he looked up at his fellow hostages and said resignedly, 'I don't think we *can* do anything but wait.'

'Yeah … but for what?' Mike muttered with an ominous glance at the other two.

———

On the drive to Tullamarine airport, Jo Modeen was happy to sit back and let Harper chat about her weekend plans and latest beau. After asking to be left at the quick drop-off point, Modeen made her way into the terminal and identified her flight's departure gate. On her way there, she stopped at a bar for a drink and sat in a quiet corner, sipping her scotch and dry while contemplating the debrief with Ben.

Her flight to the Gold Coast left on time, and she arrived at Coolangatta airport at eighteen fifty-five. She wasted no time catching a cab to her apartment. After letting herself in, she took a shower, poured herself a tall soda water with a squeeze of lime juice, and flopped onto the sofa. Sipping the refreshing drink, she picked up her private mobile from where she'd flicked it onto the coffee table, took it off flight mode, and lobbed it onto the sofa.

A second later, it vibrated violently. Twelve messages flashed, one after the other. She looked at the screen and frowned. Sighing, she dialled her mother's number.

'Mum? I just got h—'

'Josephine!' Freda gasped. 'Where have you *been*? I've been *beside* myself!'

Frowning at the panic in her mother's voice, Modeen stiffened but said evenly, 'Mum, calm down and tell me what's happened.'

'It's your father, Jo,' Freda sobbed, 'he … he's been *taken!*'

CHAPTER TWO

'Calm down, Mum. What do you mean, Dad's been taken?'

'Just that,' Freda said, sounding out of breath. 'From outside the hotel in Brisbane. The federal police are here. They think your father and two other men have been taken by a terrorist group.' Her voice broke and she sobbed, 'Oh Jo, what am I going to do?'

Modeen's mind raced. 'Stay right there, Mum. I'll arrange for Aunty Hannah to come over and be with you. I've got to make some calls, but I'll head down and see you soon. Try not to worry, I'm sure everything will be alright.' After placing a quick call to her aunt, she threw the phone onto the couch, strode to the table, and picked up her NatSec mobile. She tapped on Ben's number and listened as the dial tone hummed and buzzed.

Ben's voice when he answered was solemn. 'JD. I expected to hear from you.'

'Then you know why I'm calling, Ben.' She heard him exhale at the other end of the phone.

'Yes.' His tone grew businesslike. 'I can confirm that your father and two diplomats have been taken hostage from outside the Brisbane Hilton, where all three were staying as guests. We've viewed video footage from the hotel and believe members of a Middle Eastern terrorist organisation are responsible. This group is known to us. They call themselves "The Spear of Allah".'

When he paused, Modeen rapped, 'And?'

'We believe the terrorists hijacked the Government limo, seized the three men from the hotel, and then took them to an empty warehouse in Eagle Farm, where they changed cars. The federal police tracked the limo and found the body of the driver, one of their young officers, in the boot.'

Modeen took a breath and forced a calmness into her voice she didn't feel. 'But … why would they take Dad? He's not a diplomat.'

'Yes,' Ben said thoughtfully, 'he's the odd man out in this equation. The other two hostages are the US Deputy Secretary of State, Michael Johnston, and the British Under-Secretary of State for Foreign and Commonwealth Affairs, Sir Robert Woodrow. Both high ranking international G20 summit delegates. Somehow your father was caught up in the event, and we're assuming he was taken by accident. A case of being in the wrong place at the wrong time.'

Blowing air through tightly pursed lips, Modeen bent her head and focused on Ben's words and the reassuring timbre of his voice.

'Our intel became aware of The Spear of Allah when we were looking into Batista's dealings. Their leader, Saddam Akim, calls himself "The Scorpion". Our intel had noticed an increase in the group's activity in the lead-up to this abduction and were keeping a close eye on them. There'd been above average web activity on the G20 summit site and into the background of the attending diplomats. But of course no one could've known exactly what was being planned.'

Modeen said flatly, 'Have the terrorists made any demands?'

'Not as yet.' Ben paused. 'Look, I'd already recalled Bugs from the Middle East to help with summit security, and now I've also seconded Wolf from Delta team. Agents from MI6 and the CIA are on their way here to help with the case. I've got a meeting tomorrow morning with ASIO, followed by one with the Feds at their Melbourne headquarters, so I hope to have more information for you soon.'

'Right.'

'Now, JD, is there any point in telling you to leave this one to us? That you're too close to the event?'

Her reply was swift and decisive. 'No point at all.

This is my father we're talking about. I'm either on the case with you, or without you.'

'Yeah….' Ben sighed, and Modeen imagined him giving a resigned shake of his dark head. 'That's what I thought. Look, the Feds don't know about our recent dealings with Batista, so I'd like you and Spooky to check out his Katoomba property. It may give us a lead on where the hostages have been taken.'

'I'll contact Spooky now.'

'He'll be expecting your call.' Ben's tone softened. 'Don't worry, JD, we'll do everything in our power to get your father and the diplomats back safely.'

'I know you will, thanks Ben.' Hitting the 'call end' button on the phone, she opened the contact list and tapped on the Luke Williams entry.

Spooky answered almost immediately. 'Modeen, I'm ready to roll. Where do you want to meet?'

'I'm on the next flight to Sydney, have to drop in on Mum before we head to Katoomba.'

'How's she doing?'

'Anxious and upset, naturally. Anyway, can you pick me up from her apartment in Darling Harbour?'

'Sure, see you there around twenty-three thirty.' He ended the call.

Modeen got changed, grabbed her duffel and headed down to the basement, thumbing through her mobile's contact list as she went. NatSec's resource manager answered on the first ring.

'Leanne, I need a flight from Coolangatta to Sydney, ASAP.'

'Anything else, Jo?'

'I'll be armed, so I'll need security clearance at the airport.'

'I'll make the arrangements.'

'Thanks Leanne.' Modeen ended the call and slipped the phone into her breast pocket. Standing at the rear of her Aurion, she opened the boot, lifted the floor panel and picked up her Walther PPX. Removing the clip, she pulled back the slide and checked the breach.

Clear.

She released the slide and palmed the clip back into place. Scooping up the silencer, spare clips and night goggles, she shoved them into her duffel.

Locking and leaving her Aurion in a long-term parking bay at Coolangatta airport, she collected her ticket from the check-in counter. Seeing an airport security officer standing nearby holding a sign that read 'J Bennet', she approached him and said quietly, 'I'm Bennet.'

He looked her up and down and then studied her face for a long moment. His eyes widened and he seemed to wake from a trance. 'Driver's licence please.'

Modeen handed him her NatSec-generated Josephine Bennet licence. The officer stared at it, eyebrows raised, and then escorted her through security. Once in the departure lounge, he handed back her license with a nod. 'You have a good flight, ma'am.'

Thinking bitterly, *thanks, but I only care that it's a quick flight,* Modeen boarded her plane and arrived at Sydney's Kingsford Smith airport at twenty-two fifteen. She caught a cab to her mother's apartment in Darling Harbour and was pleased when a dressing gown-clad aunty Hannah opened the door and pulled her into a warm hug.

'Oh Jo, we're so glad to see you.'

'Hey Aunty Hann.' She gave a wan smile. 'Thanks so much for being here.' Glancing into the elegant lounge room, she saw her mother sitting pale and still on the ornate chintz sofa.

Hannah patted her hand and said softly, 'I'll make us a pot of tea.' She padded toward the kitchen in her fluffy slippers as Modeen hurried to Freda's side.

When her mother turned to her with a distraught, tear-stained face, she wrapped her arms around her, soothing, 'It's alright, Mum, I'm here.'

'Oh Jo....' Freda's voice was muffled as she sobbed against her daughter's shoulder.

Hannah came into the room a few minutes later carrying a tray. Freda sniffed and sat up as Hannah poured the tea.

'Here you go.' She handed a steaming mug to her sister and one to Modeen, who looked at her with glowing eyes.

'Thanks so much for staying with Mum.'

'Think nothing of it. What are families for, if not to be there when trouble arrives.'

They talked for a while, and when Modeen noticed her mother suppressing a yawn, she suggested she try to get some sleep. 'You too, Aunty Hann, you look tired.'

'Right, I'll clear away the dishes then hit the hay.'

'Good. I'll see you tomorrow, around mid-morning.'

Hannah contemplated her for a long moment and then nodded. 'Night, dear.'

'Night aunty Hann, sleep well.'

Modeen helped her mother to her feet and, keeping a supportive arm around her waist, walked with her into the master bedroom. After tucking her in and waiting until her breathing had slowed and deepened, Modeen crept out, closing the door behind her.

She had just flopped onto the lounge when her phone beeped with an incoming text.

Your chariot awaits.

Rising, she grabbed her duffel and headed downstairs to the idling Aurion, where Spooky sat behind the wheel patiently waiting. He glanced up as she crossed the street and made her way to the car, where she opened the back door and threw her bag onto the seat before jumping in beside him.

'Right.' He extended an arm and they fist-bumped. 'Let's do this thing.' Putting the car into gear, he accelerated onto the street and turned down Pyrmont Bridge Road, heading toward the A4 motorway.

Modeen stared moodily out the window, and then said, 'What's the latest intel on the Katoomba hacienda?'

'All seems quiet.' Spooky gave her a sideways smirk. 'After your recent "visit", they've probably abandoned the place.' He returned his gaze to the road ahead. 'But Ben reckons it's worthwhile checking it out, he's hoping we might find some clues as to where they've taken the hostages.' Pausing, he threw her a sympathetic look and said clumsily, 'Sorry … to hear that your dad's one of them.'

'Thanks Spook.' She smiled at him with her eyes. 'I'm just glad Ben's letting me help assist with this case.'

Spooky nodded, and for a time they sat quietly immersed in their own thoughts. At Strathfield, they joined the M4 and headed west toward Katoomba and the Blue Mountains.

'Did you know?' Spooky ventured, 'Ben's called Bugs back from Afghanistan. He's also seconded Wolf from Delta team.' He looked at her sideways. 'So we've just about got all the old team back for this one.'

Modeen gave a perplexed frown. 'Yeah, he told me. But pulling them off their other details is a bit extreme at this stage, don't you think?'

'You know how it goes with our old unit,' Spooky grinned. 'If one of us is in trouble, we're all in. Ben's smart, he knows there's no way he could stop Wolf from coming to help once he heard about your involvement, or Bugs for that matter. So I guess Ben figured he may as well bring 'em along.' He threw her a grin. 'Same as he knew there was no way you were going to sit this one out.'

She gave a wry snort.

'Besides, Bugs has been away for a while. This is probably a good opportunity for Ben to touch base with him. And he'll no doubt put Bugs through some training while he's here. You know, to keep him sharp.'

Some time later, Spooky slowed the Aurion and pulled off the highway, outside the driveway of the Batista hacienda.

'This is it.'

They stared at the solid wrought iron gate. It was ornately curved to complement the ostentatious white brickwork on either side of the entranceway.

Spooky turned to Modeen. 'Look familiar?'

'Not really.' She peered down the driveway. 'But then, I came at it from behind that ridge.' Pointing to the hill rising behind the property, she said, 'From the aerial photos, I'd guess the house is about eight hundred metres down the driveway.'

'OK.'

She indicated the gate with a lift of her chin. 'From the size of that padlock securing the chain around the gate and pillar, I'd reckon Ben's right about the place being deserted. And there are no lights on the control panel, or on the camera mounted on the left pillar either.'

'Yep.' Spooky opened his door. 'Wait here.' Exiting the vehicle, he strode to the gate and pressed the call button. He stood for a few moments listening, but no sound greeted him. All remained quiet. He walked back and got into the car.

'Seems like nobody's home. All the same, we shouldn't take that for granted.'

'Agreed.' Modeen shifted in her seat to fix him with an intense gaze. 'So … what's our plan of attack?'

At o-one hundred, the air was still and only a glimmer of moonlight broke the darkness. Spooky turned off the headlights and popped the boot as Modeen got out and went to the rear of the Aurion. She lifted the floor cover as he came to stand beside her. Rubbing his hands together, he picked up a Glock Seventeen, checked the breach, and handed it to her.

She raised a hand, palm forward, and murmured, 'No need, I brought Walt.'

'Oh, right. Of course.' He grinned at her and pushed the Glock muzzle-first into the back of his pants.

While he got busy assembling the Vanquish sniper rifle, Modeen grabbed the MP5, checked the breach, palmed a full magazine into its base and fitted the silencer. Opening the car's back door, she unzipped her duffel and retrieved the Walther PPX and night vision goggles. She tucked 'Walt' into a holster and slipped it over her shoulder.

Spooky finished assembling the sniper rifle and laid it on the back seat. Returning to the boot, he rested a foot on the rear moulded bumper and strapped a bayonet to his lower leg. He then opened the tool kit compartment, pulled out a pair of bolt cutters, donned his night vision goggles, and strode to the gate.

Taking a closer look at it, he muttered, 'They've chained it closed. Must mean the power's definitely off, or been cut. Otherwise why bother with the chain.'

Hearing the rasp of metal slicing through metal as he cut off the lock, Modeen slipped on her night vision goggles and helped him slide the heavy single gate open. They jumped back in the car and drove slowly down the gravel driveway, lights off, using their goggles to see the way ahead and scan the surroundings for signs of activity.

When the gravel track veered right and took a gentle decline through a shallow gully, Spooky brought the car to a rolling stop. Peering ahead, they could just make out the house, a dark, rectangular silhouette against the side of the hill. Opening the centre console compartment, Spooky pulled out a box and handed it to Modeen. It contained two small comms units. She took one and handed him the other.

Switching off the interior light, Spooky nodded to Modeen and they exited the vehicle. Moving swiftly but quietly, he grabbed a backpack and the sniper rifle from off the back seat. As he headed up the rise to the left of the vehicle, Modeen collected the MP5 and, keeping to the deepest shadows, proceeded across the gully toward the hacienda that had been Batista's home.

Once in position on the rise, Spooky pressed an index finger to his ear and said softly, 'Comms check.'

Modeen halted and sank to her haunches, whispering, 'Check, five by five. What's the view like from up there, Spook?'

'Pretty good. Looks quiet.' He pressed a button on the rifle's scope, changing it to thermal imaging. 'No heat signatures either. You're clear all the way to the house.'

'Copy that.'

'Take your time, we're not in a hurry.'

She rose but kept low as she moved forward, hugging the left of the gravel driveway. A hundred metres from the homestead, the track narrowed to traverse a culvert made from heavy railway sleepers. Pausing there, she adjusted her night vision goggles and was about to continue when she felt the hairs on the back of her neck stiffen.

Something was wrong.

Squatting, she peered along the track, scanning left to right, checking and double-checking the way ahead and behind. When her goggles revealed a razor-thin dark line across the road ahead, she thought at first it was a glitch or static in the goggles. She scanned again, this time homing in on the line.

Spooky's voice came through her earpiece. 'What's up?' He was watching from his vantage point.

She pressed her ear and muttered, 'Tripwire.'

'Nice going! I see that radar of yours hasn't lost its edge.' He paused, and then said drily, 'And nice of them to put out the welcome mat for us.'

'Yeah.'

His tone grew serious again. 'Hold your position I'll be right there.' Making his way back down the rise to the car, he grabbed a compact aerosol can from out of the boot and crept to where Modeen sat waiting. When he used the spray to mark the location of the tripwire, the fluorescent paint stood out like a beacon through the night vision goggles.

He threw her a nod, and they stepped warily over the tripwire and advanced toward the house. Reverting to hand signals, she waved him to the right as she moved toward the left side of the building. They made their way under the white brick archways and onto the veranda at the front.

Everything was still and no sound penetrated the early morning gloom.

The huge front room spanned the full width of the hacienda. She could see Spooky peering in a window on the far side. She switched on the laser sight of her MP5 and pointed it at the front door, dancing the little red dot around the door handle. Seeing the small parcel of C4 explosives moulded there, he gave her the thumbs up.

Pulling the bayonet from its scabbard, he reached up to jimmy open the window in front of him, when Modeen broke comms silence to hiss, 'Stop! Window on your right is clear.'

He froze, backed away and moved to his right, mouthing, 'Thank you,' at her. After prizing open the window she'd indicated and slipping inside, he peered down the long central hallway, and then moved across the room toward the far wall, checking the windows until he found one he could open for Modeen.

Once she was inside, they slung their rifles and took out their hand guns. Advancing down the hall-way, back to back, they covered each other's six as they rotated past each door. The first doors off to the left and right were closed. Pointing a hand down the corri-dor, Modeen indicated they move on to the next. She slid past the opening of the third and paused at the entrance. Keeping low, Spooky moved swiftly into the room at a forty-five degree angle, his Glock leading the way. She followed him in on the opposite forty-five, and found herself in a good-sized bedroom.

Clear.

When they moved on to the next, another spacious bedroom, it too was empty. They entered the last room to the left. Clearly the main bedroom, it sported a king-sized four poster bed and a sunken floor. A jacuzzi sat silently in one corner of the room, beside which large glass doors gave a view to the veranda space and out past the white brick arches.

Clear.

They backed into the hallway and continued to the elaborate but grimy open-plan kitchen. Dirty dishes were stacked in the sink, and the bin's stinking, fly-blown contents had overflowed onto the floor. Holding her breath, Modeen checked it was clear and then hurried past and into the next room.

It was an expansive games room sporting a large pool table and an elaborate mirror-lined bar. It too was grubby and littered with empties. Moving silently, she went to the double doors and peered out at the paved pool area. When Spooky tapped her on the shoulder, she gave a start. He pointed to the doors, made a fist and then flicked all his fingers apart to indicate an explosion. Taking his meaning, she looked at the doors and saw more C4 moulded around the handles. She threw him a grateful nod.

While she went to check behind the bar, Spooky waited for her at the hallway entrance, and then they made their way back to the two closed rooms. He stopped outside one of the doors and raised a fist in a halting gesture. When she paused behind him, he indicated his backpack with a thumb.

Pointing to the closed doors, he pressed his earpiece and whispered, 'Could be wired.'

Reaching inside his pack, she took out two small charges, each about the size of a matchbox, and handed one to him. After they'd secured the charges next to the handle of each door, she set the built-in timers for ten seconds and, at his nod, hit the start buttons. They retreated swiftly down the hallway and took cover in the kitchen as, with a wall-shattering bang, both doors blew off their hinges and landed in the middle of their respective rooms.

Glancing toward Spooky, Modeen said, 'Well I guess if anyone were here, they would've heard that.'

At his nod, they made their way to the two now doorless rooms. She entered the one on the right while Spooky checked the one on the left. After only a few moments they met again in the hallway.

'All clear.'

'Mine too.'

'Looks like they packed up and bugged out.'

'Yeah, they haven't left anything for us.' Spooky frowned. 'Makes you wonder why they went to all that trouble with the booby traps.' He flicked a thumb over his shoulder at the room he'd just checked. 'Looks like that was the study, there's a desk and filing cabinet, but not a skerrick of paper left in it.'

Modeen eyed him thoughtfully. 'Well, we're here, we may as well make a thorough job of searching the place. You take a closer look inside and I'll check out the back.' Going into the front room again, she climbed through the open window and made her way around to the pool area. Passing the spa, she noticed dried blood stains on the pavement behind it.

Batista's blood....

She recalled the image of him forcing the maid's head underwater. If she hadn't taken him out the young woman would've died, there was no doubt about that. Modeen looked up at the ridge from where she'd taken the shot. Shapes were starting to form on the landscape. The sun would be coming up soon.

Heading into the gloomy back yard, she spotted a derelict wooden shed in the furthest corner, and walked over to it. When she opened the rickety wooden doors, she spied a rusted old Ford pickup inside. She tried the passenger side door and was pleased to find it unlocked. It gave a resounding creak when she opened it, and empty booze cans rattled out and onto the ground at her feet.

She froze, listening keenly as the cans settled and silence fell again. All stayed quiet.

With a click of her tongue, she checked the inside of the cab and found only fast food wrappers and more empty cans. Opening the glove box, she found a nest of papers and pulled them out. With a quick glance at their contents, she bundled them into her back pocket and returned to the house, where she met Spooky in the games room.

'House is clean,' he announced. 'How'd you go?'

'Found these papers in an old pickup in the shed.' She pulled them out of her pocket and spread them on the bar.

He thumbed through them one by one, examining

their contents through his night vision goggles. 'Hmm … the rest are crap, but these might be useful.' He separated two documents and waved one at Modeen. 'One expired rego paper for …,' and he threw her a significant glance, '… one Salvatore Batista … now deceased.' Grinning at her indifferent shrug of one shoulder, he went on. 'With a Brisbane PO Box as the address. And the other …,' and he waved the second paper in the air, '… an old mooring slip for a berth at Scarborough boat harbour, also in Brisbane.'

'Right.' Modeen gave a brisk nod. 'So, should we leave the place like we found it?'

'Why not? We might get lucky, they might forget about the booby traps and trip wire and blow themselves up.'

She gave a snort. 'Where to now, Spook? We're wasting our time here.'

'We'll head back to Sydney. I've arranged a two bedroom apartment near Darling Harbour. We might be able to get in a couple of hour's sleep if we're lucky. Then I'll drop you off at your mum's and report to Ben. Depending on what he's found, we'll go from there.' They made their way to the open window as Spooky added, 'I know he's meeting with ASIO and the Feds at o-nine hundred, but he might even have some new intel before that. His contacts at Pine Gap are pretty thorough.'

CHAPTER FOUR

In the gloom of the early morning, a blue-hulled trawler entered Dickson's Inlet in far north Queensland. With its motor working at just above idle, the boat chugged through the darkness with only the dull glow of its navigation lights illuminating the way along the inlet and into Packers Creek.

The three men in the front hold were jerked awake by the sound of heavy footsteps coming down the stairs toward them. When the door to the hold was wrenched open, they blinked and shaded their eyes from the harsh strobing light of a powerful torch.

Azeez stood in the doorway shining the light into their faces. 'Up you dogs!' he ordered. 'On your feet.'

Wincing, the hostages groaned as they rose from the tattered bunks. Their bones ached from lying on the makeshift lumpy bedding. Azeez entered the hold and herded the men out and into the narrow corridor. All four lurched sideways as the trawler came to a sudden stop and bumped against a solid mooring.

Azeez regained his balance quickly and yelled, 'Move!'

John Modeen led the procession up the stairs and onto the deck of the trawler, where they were met by Aldin and two other men. John's eyes were still recovering from having been dazzled by the torchlight, and he strained to see in the darkness. When he caught the toe of a shoe in a haphazardly coiled length of thick, slimy rope, he fell heavily to the timber deck landing on all fours, and was reefed to his feet by the collar of his overalls.

Shoved onto a makeshift gangway leading to a jetty, he glanced over his shoulder and saw his comrades shuffling close behind. A guard prodded him in the side and he stumbled onto the jetty. Peering through the dim hint of early morning light, he could just make out the path ahead, leading through thick mangroves.

He jumped at the sound of a startled grunt and a cry of 'Ah!' behind him. Turning, he saw Sir Robert Woodrow stumble over his own feet and fall to the ground with a thud. The slope and his rotund shape had him rolling off the path into the marshes amid shouts from the guards. As Aldin and the others rushed over to seize a winded Sir Robert and drag him to his feet, John took a hasty glance around and found himself unguarded.

Thinking this was his chance, that if he could get

away, he could alert the authorities and hopefully save the other two hostages, he spun on his heels and took off down the path.

For an older man, John Modeen was still in good condition. Hearing shouts of alarm behind him, he gained speed and burst out of the trees lining the track, only to be tackled and knocked off his feet by a guard lurking in the shadows beside the path.

Later, when he regained consciousness, he was lying on the floor inside a dark room. He hurt all over and his head was still spinning, but he opened his eyes to see Sir Robert kneeling at his side staring into his face.

Realising he was conscious, Woodrow said jovially, 'Jolly good effort, old man.'

'Shut up!' He was silenced with a stinging slap to the back of the head, and shoved out of the way.

John screwed up his eyes as blinding torchlight filled his vision and another voice with a very Australian accent said, 'Nice try, Modeen, though foolish.' The man behind the voice moved closer, and a blinking John was able to make out some of his facial features as he continued speaking. His voice was smooth and even, as though chatting about the weather. 'Stunts like that will get you killed sooner rather than later. So it would be wise to make that one your last.'

As the man spoke, John concentrated on making

out his face. He squinted, thinking there was something familiar about it.

But where would he have seen him before, this Aussie terrorist?

———

At o-eight hundred, Spooky dropped Modeen at her mother's ritzy apartment in Darling Harbour. Hannah, still in her dressing gown and slippers, opened the door to her knock.

The warm aroma of toast and percolated coffee wafted out of the doorway as she said kindly, 'Jo, good morning dear. You look tired.' They hugged and then went inside. Hannah headed to the kitchen. 'Just making some breakfast.' She glanced at her niece's drawn, pale face. 'Looks like you could use a good meal.'

'Thanks Aunty Hann.' Modeen gave a weak smile. 'How's Mum this morning?'

Hannah's expression grew concerned. 'Still asleep when I checked on her a little while ago. I didn't want to wake her.'

Modeen nodded slowly. 'Want a hand with breakfast?'

'No, thanks dear. You just relax, it's almost done.'

Seeing the dining table already spread with place mats, cutlery and condiments, Modeen left her aunt to carry on, knowing Hannah would prefer to be busy so as not to dwell on her brother-in-law's fate. Sighing and running a hand over her forehead, she went out onto the balcony. Resting her arms on the railing, she looked across to Sydney Harbour bridge, without really seeing it. She stayed there, pondering the morning's mission, until her aunt called that breakfast was ready. Straightening, she took a deep breath and went back inside.

'I can't stick around for too long, Aunty Hann.'

'Don't worry dear, I can stay with your mother for the rest of the week, or …,' and she threw Modeen an anxious glance, '… as long as it takes 'til this mess is sorted out.' She put on a brave smile. 'Now, here's your breakfast. Eat up.'

With a flourish, she put a large dinner plate in front of Modeen. In the centre of the fine white china, two perfectly poached eggs, garnished with a sprig of parsley, sat on a thick buttered slice of toast.

'Coffee?' She threw her niece a smile.

'Yes please, white with one.'

'No, they'd bugged out.' Spooky was in his car on videoconference with Ben. 'They had the place rigged with explosive charges on the front and back doors and some of the windows, and even had a tripwire rigged across the driveway.'

'Did you find anything that might give us a lead?' Ben asked.

'Modeen found some paperwork that might be useful, in an old pickup parked in a shed out the back of the homestead. There's a registration paper for Salvatore Batista with a Brisbane PO box address.'

'Box number?'

'555. The other paper is a mooring receipt from Scarborough Boat Harbour, for berth number….' Unfolding the creased and faded receipt, he scanned its details. '… H17.'

'Good work.'

Spooky smiled and nodded. 'Thanks. All in a day's – or should that be night's – work!'

'How's JD holding up?'

'She's doing OK, considering she must be under a fair bit of pressure with her father's life on the line. She's at her mum's apartment at the moment.'

'Her performance hasn't been affected?'

'Nah, she's as sharp as ever. I was lucky to have her along. As we all know, once she's on the job she's tenacious and totally focused.'

'Good. Wolf has just arrived, so I'll send him up to Brisbane to check out the boat harbour. Once I get a residential address for that PO box, I'll get him to follow up on that too. I want you both to rendezvous with him there in case this leads somewhere.'

Spooky nodded. 'Right, so we'll fly to the Gold Coast, collect Modeen's car, and head up to Brisbane to meet him. Here's hoping he finds something. If not, where do we go from there?'

'I might have some more information after this morning's meeting.'

'Right. I'll organise some flights, collect Modeen and we'll be on our way. Cheers.' Spooky ended the call and then hit another number on his contact list.

'Reece here.'

Spooky's tone was businesslike when he said, 'Need two seats on the next available flight from Sydney to Coolangatta for Luke Williams and Josephine Bennet.'

He heard Reece grunt and tap on a keyboard, and then the young man said, 'There's a Virgin flight leaving in fifteen minutes … or a Qantas fight leaving in ninety.'

'Qantas,' Spooky rapped, 'and we'll be armed.'

'Sure, I'll arrange security clearance. And your tickets will be waiting for you at the Qantas check-in counter. Have a good flight.'

'Cheers.' Spooky ended the call and then sent a text to Modeen.

Flight to Gold Coast in 90 minutes.

Modeen checked her watch. Her mother hadn't woken yet. 'I have to go now, Aunty Hann.' She pulled her in for a goodbye hug and kissed her aunt on a rose-watered, wrinkled cheek.

'Take care, love. I'll let your mum know you came by.'

'Thanks … for everything.' Throwing her a warm smile, Modeen went out, closing the door behind her. She crossed the road and found Spooky waiting for her in his Aurion.

He started the car as she jumped into the passenger's seat. 'Right to go?' At her nod, he nosed out of the parking spot and accelerated onto the street. 'I've organised flights to Coolangatta. We'll pick up your car and drive to Brisbane. Wolf will meet us at the airport there.'

Wolf.

An image flashed before her eyes, of the last time she'd seen Troy Wolverton. She'd lain in bed, curled in the indent that was still warm from his body, saying nothing, watching him dress and throw the last few things into his duffel. She'd risen to see him off, but they still didn't speak as he made his way toward the door of the Meriton apartment, about to head to the airport for his flight to Perth.

Holding his bag in one large, strong hand, he'd stopped in the apartment's doorway to turn and gaze at her for a long moment, an unreadable expression in his dark eyes. Finally, throwing her a nod and a lopsided grin, he'd said low and soft, 'I'll see ya, Mrs Ryan,' before striding out.

Swallowing and blinking away the image, she stared straight ahead and said, 'Right then, Spooky, let's go.'

Wolf strode out of Brisbane airport, hire car keys jingling in his hand. He located the unremarkable white Holden sedan, threw his bag in the back and his leather jacket on the passenger seat, and got in behind the wheel. Wasting no time, he entered 'Scarborough boat harbour' into the GPS and as soon as the directions appeared on the screen, started the car and drove off with a cursory squeal of tyres.

He drove confidently through the congested city traffic, his hands easy on the wheel, and got to the marina in good time. Parking out the front, he switched off the ignition and sat in the car, scanning the area and thinking, *seen one marina, you've seen 'em all.* Apart from a few salty types mooching around their yachts and launches, all was calm. Throwing on his jacket to cover the bulge of his shoulder holster, he got out of the car and sauntered to the marina office.

The elderly lady behind the counter looked up when he entered, and smiled. 'Hello there, young man. Can I help you?'

His lips tipped upward at the 'young man' reference. 'I'm here to meet someone. Said his boat's berthed at H17?'

'Oh, I see.' The lady picked up a map showing the marina layout and ran a finger over one of the many arms bristling with berths. 'H17 ... oh yeah, the Passagemaker Bluewater trawler.' She glanced up at

Wolf. 'But she's not 'ere, they took 'er out yesterday morning.' Her eyes narrowed. 'Say, are you looking at buying 'er?' She pointed to the noticeboard on her left. 'She's a fine solid vessel, and a good price too.'

Wolf went over to stand in front of the noticeboard. 'Which one is it?'

'On the left, in the middle. With the dark blue hull.'

'Right.' He peered at it, committing its details to memory. 'Any idea where they were headed?' He threw her a smile while taking out his mobile and snapping a photo of the advertisement. With a few deft finger strokes, he texted the photo to Ben.

She shook her head. 'They didn't say. But I do know they purchased a lot of fuel, so I doubt you'll see 'em back for a while. Those Passagemakers are a good, reliable long range cruiser.'

Thinking with amusement that she was a good person to have on side if ever he had a boat to sell, Wolf thanked her and then said, 'Just one more thing. Could I have a copy of the berth layout?'

'Sure, here ya go.'

Taking the map from her, he dipped his head. 'Thanks ma'am.' Folding the map, he slipped it into a jacket pocket. 'Hope you don't mind if I have a little look around while I'm here?'

'Not at all.' She smiled winningly at him. 'And once you've got your vessel, we can do you a good deal on a mooring.'

With another polite nod at the obliging lady, he

strode out of the office. Taking care to stroll noncha-lantly, he made his way down to the wharf and stopped by H17. He was staring into the empty berth, pondering where the abductors might have gone, when his phone buzzed and vibrated in his pocket.

He accepted the call and barked, 'Ryan.'

Ben also didn't waste time with pleasantries. 'Got your text and passed it onto Bryan in Intel, well done. JD and Spooky are on their way, so sit tight. If we get a lead on that trawler, I want you all ready to roll.'

'Copy that.'

'The lead on the PO box went nowhere,' Ben went on. 'It was linked to a residential address in Barclay Street, Southgate, but it's unlikely to be a place of inter-est. Batista sold the property ten years ago to a couple from Melbourne, who sold it five years later to a retired cattle farmer from Biloela.'

Wolf nodded into the phone. 'Anything come out of your meeting this mornin'?'

'Not much.' Mild amusement crept into Ben's tone. 'But the Feds were a bit red-faced. I think they got their arses reamed over the abductions. They're busy ramping up security arrangements for the G20, but MI6 and the CIA aren't taking any more chances. They're sending over extra agents, reckon they don't want anyone else disappearing.'

'Do they know the reason for the abductions?'

'They're pretty sure it'll be an exchange deal. The US army is holding two senior members of a guerrilla group captured during a mission in Iraq. They're expecting the "Spear of Allah" to demand their release in return for the hostages.'

Wolf frowned. 'What are the chances the three will come out of this alive?' He heard Ben exhale at the end of the phone.

'I think we both know the answer to that. Look, we just have to find them. I'll be in touch as soon as I hear more.'

The phone went silent, but soon after buzzed and vibrated again.

'Wolf? It's Spooky. We'll be in Brisbane in an hour. Where do you wanna meet?'

'Hey Spook. I'm headin' back to Brisbane airport now to drop off the hire car.'

'Cool, see you there.'

As Wolf snapped his phone shut and turned to make his way back to the car, a pair of eyes watched his every movement with great interest.

Modeen and Spooky arrived at Brisbane airport and nosed the Aurion into the quick pick-up lane, where they saw Wolf standing on the sidewalk, duffel slung across his broad shoulders. When they pulled into the curb in front of him, he promptly opened the back door, threw his bag onto the seat and slid in beside it.

Nodding a greeting at them, he muttered drily, 'You guys had lunch?'

Returning his nod but keeping her eyes forward, Modeen nosed the car back into the traffic, as Spooky grinned at Wolf. 'Excellent idea, mate. Where to?'

'I passed a pub on my way here. It's not far away.'

'Sounds like a plan. What's it called?'

'The Royal Hotel.'

Reaching forward, Spooky punched the name into the Aurion's built-in GPS, while Modeen negotiated the busy airport traffic, and Wolf updated them on his conversation with Ben.

'The PO box you guys found led to a dead end, but I managed to get a photo of the trawler Batista had at the boat harbour. Ben's puttin' the word out on it. He wants us to sit tight 'til they get a lead on its whereabouts.'

Leaning forward, Wolf put a hand on Modeen's shoulder. 'Sorry to hear your Dad's been dragged into this, Modeen.'

She didn't speak, but threw him a grateful sideways glance.

Turning off Sandgate Road, Modeen pulled the Aurion into the carpark at the rear of the Royal Hotel. She switched off the engine and glanced at the two men, announcing matter-of-factly, 'I think we picked up a tail.'

'Red Nissan Navara?' Spooky looked over his shoulder as a red dual cab ute sailed past.

'That's the one.'

'Yeah, we picked him up as soon as we left the airport.' He threw Wolf a wink. 'Must've followed you from the marina.'

Wolf scowled. 'Can't say I noticed anyone tailing me. Must be losin' my touch.' He peered into the rear view mirror and watched the dual cab drive past again and park on the opposite side of the road. 'Looks like only one in the car … reckon we should nab him?'

'No.' Spooky reached into a breast pocket and

pulled out a small metal disc about the size of a five cent piece. He held it between thumb and forefinger and waved it at them. 'I reckon we should track him, might give us a lead.'

Modeen gave a brisk nod. 'Agreed. So how do you want to do this?'

He grinned. 'Well ... I don't know about you guys, but I could go a nice char-grilled rump.'

Wolf's initially perplexed expression cleared, and he smacked his lips. 'Me too.'

'And me.' Modeen smiled. 'Right, looks like three steaks then.'

They got out of the car and strolled casually toward the hotel, entering through the rear door. As Spooky slipped out the front, Wolf and Modeen made their way to the dining room and sat at a booth on the far wall.

The man in the red dual cab got out and walked to the hotel's back entrance, swarthy hands tucked into the pockets of his threadbare jeans, glancing every now and then over his hunched shoulders. Looking around to make sure he was alone, he pulled a mobile phone from his pocket and hit the speed dial. His call was answered almost immediately.

'I followed the big guy to the airport,' he mumbled through tense lips. 'He was picked up by another man and a woman in a dark-coloured sedan....' He flicked a glance at the parked Aurion. 'Yeah, looks official to me.' After pausing to listen, he went on. 'Nah, they didn't see me. Just drove to a pub on Sandgate Road. That's where we are now.'

He paused again. 'Why do you want to know what they look like? What difference does that make?' This time when he listened, he frowned and raised a defensive hand. 'Alright, alright. No need to shout. They look like you a bit … well, the blokes do anyway. But all three got the same haircut as you. The woman's blonde and not a bad looker. The second guy's short, but pretty fit I'd reckon, same as the other two.' He listened again. 'Do you want me to follow them inside?' Hearing the response, he rolled his eyes. 'What? Why am I in danger? They don't know I'm here. I could go in—' He winced. 'No, I understand—' Hanging his head, he growled, 'I *said* I understand. I'm leaving. Yes, right now. And I'll make sure I'm not followed.'

Sauntering in from the front of the hotel, Spooky joined Modeen and Wolf in the dining area. Sliding into the booth beside Modeen, he said in an undertone, 'Done. If he's still there when we're ready to go, we might have to lose him in the traffic and hope he returns to the nest.'

'Good one.' Modeen pushed a schooner of beer in front of him. 'You're a great sneak, Spook.'

'Ta.' Spooky dipped his head at her, winked and raised his glass high in a toast. 'Who Dares Wins!'

All three clinked glasses. They took a long, thirsty drink, and then Modeen set down her glass. Resting her elbows on the table, she leaned closer to the other two. 'So far we know that the abductors took the three to a shed in Eagle Farm, where they were transferred into a white Transit van. We also know that the trawler's departure coincided with the abductions, so it's a fair bet they're on it.' She straightened and ran a hand through her razor-cut blonde hair.

Following her lead, Wolf kept his voice low. 'Only problem is, the trawler could be anywhere from the tip of Cape York to the bottom of Tassie.'

Seeing her quick frown, Spooky put a hand on her shoulder. 'Don't worry Modeen, we'll find 'em. If we're lucky, "old mate" in the red dual cab might lead us straight to 'em, or give us some new intel on where they're being held.'

A waitress approached their booth carrying three plates heaped with chips, salad and char-grilled steaks.

Spooky glanced at Modeen. 'You ordered for me?'

Wolf replied, 'I did.'

'Medium-rare with pepper sauce?'

Wolf rolled his eyes. 'What do you take me for, some kind of idiot? You've only been havin' steaks like that ever since I've *known* you.'

'Cheers, big fella.' Spooky grinned. 'You'll make someone a good wife one day.'

. . .

After finishing their meals, they headed out to the carpark.

The red dual cab had gone.

Modeen clicked the remote to unlock the Aurion and Spooky went around to sit in the front passenger's seat. He pressed a small button above the glove box and a thin computer screen slid out, rotated and came to rest vertically in front of him. Putting the palm of his hand on the screen, he logged into the NatSec network, tapped on a GPS icon, and typed in a code.

Glancing at Modeen, he muttered, 'Old mate's heading south on Wardell Street.'

Modeen started the car and the Aurion's powerful V6 engine roared into life. She turned to gaze at Spooky and then at Wolf. 'We ready?'

Spooky patted the left side of his chest, dipped his head and threw her a wink. Wolf kept his gaze focused out the window, but casually reached up to open the left side of his jacket, revealing a matt black Glock seventeen nestled in a leather shoulder holster.

'Right.' Modeen put the car into gear and pulled out of the carpark with only the smallest scrabble of tyres on the gravel covering the bitumen.

'Head north onto Kedron Park Road, then west onto Stafford.' Spooky peered at the GPS. 'Looks like he's pulled into a driveway in Vincent Street in Enoggera.'

The traffic was heavy as they cruised along Stafford Road.

'Now left onto South Pine Road, and stay on it. It turns into Wardell Street after crossing Samford.' After a few minutes, he announced, 'Vincent coming up on your right.'

Modeen turned into the old, established street. It was dotted with purple flowering jacaranda trees and orange-red flowering poincianas. Most of the homes were high-set weatherboard Queenslanders, many of them recently renovated. Some of the gardens were well tended, others ragged and overgrown. In the distance a bored dog could be heard yapping half-heartedly.

'Slow down ...,' Spooky said, '... it should be just up here, on the left past Noeline Street.' He pointed through the windscreen to his left and Modeen nosed the car tight against the curb a couple of houses back from the corner. He hit the button and the screen retracted neatly into the dash.

They left the vehicle and walked casually up the rise past Noeline Street, slowing to a dawdle when a red Nissan Navara came into view. It was parked in a carport alongside an old Holden sedan. The house was another weatherboard Queenslander, high-set with a wooden flight of stairs leading onto an expansive front porch. Another sedan was parked sideways across the unkempt front yard.

Modeen lifted her chin at Wolf. 'You take the back. Spook and I'll take the front. We'll go on your signal.'

Wolf nodded and made his way through the open carport, past the still-warm red Nissan. The others gave him two minutes before walking up the pathway to the front of the house.

Wolf stole down the far side of the building. The windows were set high so he didn't need to duck past them. The rambling house extended an impressive distance down the narrow allotment. He reached the back and saw a flight of steps leading to a small landing in front of a solid rear door. Pausing at the base, he looked at his watch.

At the front of the house, Modeen and Spooky crept up the stairs and stood on each side of the front door. Modeen reached out a tentative hand and tried the door nob.

It turned easily.

She nodded to Spooky and they held their breath, waiting silently for Wolf's signal. Moments later, they felt the house shake and heard a pounding of feet as Wolf thumped up the back stairs.

He didn't slow when he reached the landing. Kicking the heavy back door off its hinges with a splintering crash, he burst inside.

CHAPTER SIX

The whole house vibrated and erupted into a frenzy of yells and stomping feet as its startled inhabitants scurried into frantic action.

Flinging open the front door, Modeen threw Spooky a quick nod. Keeping low, he dashed inside and across the wide front corridor at a forty-five degree angle, and disappeared through an archway off to the right. Modeen hung back on the porch, out of sight from those within. Through the wooden floorboards under her feet, she felt the pounding of a heavy-set man running in her direction.

She braced herself, pressing her back flat against the front wall of the house. The floorboards visibly shook as the big man burst through the doorway, looking over his shoulder to see if he was being pursued. Leaping forward, she struck him in the side with a hip and shoulder, using just enough force to veer him off course. He staggered across the porch and crashed headlong into a pillar with an explosive grunt as the air was punched out of his lungs.

When he slipped unconscious to the deck, Modeen pulled out her Walther PPX and stepped over to grab him by the collar of his greasy jacket. With a quick look around to see if anyone on the street had noticed the commotion, she proceeded to drag the unconscious man inside, keeping the cocked PPX in her leading hand.

In classic Queenslander style, a central corridor ran the full length of the house's interior, and most of the rooms opened off it. Wolf stood at the far end, in the laundry doorway. The rear door he'd kicked in lay askew on the floor behind him. It was almost in two pieces, fractured from top to bottom.

He was about to move when two large, bare-chested men emerged suddenly from the closest room to his left. The front man let out a deep growl and charged toward Wolf, arms outstretched and big hands tensed and claw-like. The second man pulled up behind him, head bent, struggling with the mechanism of his Browning nine millimetre pistol.

Seeing them, Wolf instantly crouched before lunging forward and thrusting his right foot into the chest of the advancing man. The impact lifted his assailant off the floor and threw him back into his companion, sending them both crashing to the floor. The other man was still wrestling with the Browning but managed to fire off a shot as he fell. The shot echoed loudly as the bullet tore through the ceiling, dislodging a cloud of plaster.

Coughing and shaking powdery chunks of plaster off his head, Wolf reached for his Glock as a third man came crashing into the corridor backwards. With a grunt of pain, the man slammed, back-first, into the wall. Staggering, he tried to raise the Smith and Wesson thirty-eight revolver he was holding, but it slipped from his hand as his head rocked violently backward. As the man slumped lifeless to the floor, Spooky stepped into the corridor, smoke curling from the silencer of his Glock.

The man with the Browning, still pinned beneath the dead weight of his winded companion, had managed to wriggle his gun hand free. Seeing him raise the weapon, Spooky fired off another round, and the man's pistol fell to the floor with a thud as his body went limp.

'I don't think we'll have much time before the cops get here,' Modeen barked as she dragged her unconscious assailant down the corridor toward them. Spooky hastened forward to grab the opposite collar of the man's jacket. Together they hauled him into the kitchen.

Wolf bent to grab the first guy he'd kicked, only to have the man reach up and seize him around the throat. Throwing up both his arms to break the hold, Wolf stepped forward and landed a hard right cross, shattering the man's nose. This time, when he bent to grab the guy by the hair, he was met with only a full body flinch and a pathetic moan of resistance.

When Wolf dragged him over his two dead companions and into the kitchen, Modeen spun a chair around and Wolf shoved the bleeding man onto it.

She threw Spooky a nod and he said, 'Right, I'll do a quick search,' and disappeared from the room.

The man sat hunched in the chair, groaning, legs sprawled straight out in front of him. His head lolled forward and blood dripped from his nose onto the scuffed black and white linoleum at his feet. Modeen ripped a length of cord from the dusty venetian blinds at the kitchen window and bound his hands behind the chair.

Wolf leaned in to growl in the man's ear, 'Where are the hostages?'

The man spat bloodied saliva onto the floor and spoke into his chest. 'Don't know nothin' about any hostages.'

Modeen stepped forward to shove Walt's silencer hard into his temple. 'Where are they?'

He threw her a filthy look out of one eye, the other was swelling closed. 'I told you, I don't know what you're talkin' about.' His broken nose made his voice nasal, but there was no denying his sullen tone.

'Last chance.' Wolf leaned closer to glare into the man's bloodshot eyes. 'WHERE ARE THE HOSTAGES?'

The man's lips twisted. 'You *simple* or somethink? I *said* I *don't know* nothink.'

Wolf stood back and lifted his foot. When he brought it crashing down on top of the man's left knee, the joint broke and gave away with a sickening sound of cracking bone and tearing sinew. The man gave a shriek of pain and jerked convulsively against his bonds, his face contorted and slick with sweat and blood. When he opened his eyes, his tortured gaze fell on his left leg and he screamed again. The unnatural angle of his meaty left calf and foot made it appear they were no longer part of him.

'WHERE ARE THEY?' Wolf roared over the man's cries of agony.

Wincing, the man blinked and risked a glance at Wolf. What he saw made him sniff back the blood in his nose, swallow and choke, 'H-headed north ... by b-boat.'

'WHERE north?'

'I don't know!' the man sobbed. Tears of pain rolled down his cheeks and into his gaping, tortured mouth.

Gripping the man's face in vicelike hands, Wolf stared at him, eyeball to eyeball, and snarled, 'TALK! Or I'll break the other one.'

First pleading, 'NO! Please, no,' and then yelping, 'NORTH!' the man broke down and bawled, 'That's all I know. Up north ... somewhere ... I don't know where.'

Wolf released his hold and the man's head sagged

to his chest as he continued openly weeping. After staring narrow-eyed at his prisoner for a long moment, Wolf muttered, 'This idiot's no more use to us. Just a brainless goon only told the bare minimum.' With a lift of his stubbled chin, he indicated the guy Modeen had dragged in. 'What about "fat boy"? Can we make him talk?'

She stiffened and hissed, 'No time! I hear sirens.' Glancing at the inert man at her feet, she said, 'And "fat boy" is still unconscious. Let's go, we'll leave these guys for the Feds.'

Wolf swore under his breath. 'Shouldn't we take 'em with us? The Feds won't get anything outta them, but give us time—'

'No, we've gotta go.' She grabbed his sleeve. 'C'mon. Don't forget, these guys popped a Federal officer.'

'Oh yeah.' Wolf gave an evil grin. 'That almost makes it OK.' He followed Modeen as she led the way out of the kitchen, shouting, 'Spook! We're leaving. NOW.'

He strode out of one of the rooms carrying a laptop computer and followed them to the front door. They went down the stairs and out onto the sidewalk, where they casually made their way to the Aurion.

Police cars screamed past, sirens blaring, as Modeen pulled away from the curb. She turned into Noeline Street before doubling back onto the main road. In the passenger's seat beside her, Spooky pulled his phone out of a shirt pocket and dialled Ben.

When his call was answered, he announced calmly, 'Vincent Street, Enoggera, Brisbane. Police are at the scene, you might want to get the Feds there ASAP.' He paused briefly. 'We didn't get much time to interrogate the insurgents before the cops showed up, but have reason to believe the hostages are being taken north by boat.' He nodded. 'Right,' and hung up. Turning to the others, he said, 'Ben's informing the Feds and alerting all NatSec contacts north of Brisbane.' The other two nodded their understanding as he opened the laptop. When the screen came to life, he grunted. 'Password protected … of course.'

'Hey,' Modeen threw over her shoulder, 'try, *Spear of Allah*, all one word.'

Spooky looked at her doubtfully but said, 'OK' and typed the word into the login screen. The computer gave a disapproving beep, and he muttered, 'No good.'

Wolf leaned into the gap between the two front seats. 'Try just *Allah*.'

Spooky rolled his eyes, then shrugged. 'Worth a try,' and he typed it in. 'Well, buggar me, it worked! The boy's good.'

Modeen threw Wolf a grin and he slouched against the seat with a self-satisfied smirk. Putting his hands behind his head, he gazed out the window as Spooky got busy tapping on the keyboard and clicking through folders. Modeen pulled into the nearest shopping centre carpark and left the motor running with the air conditioner on. She yanked on the parking brake and then leaned toward Spooky, straining to get a clear view of the laptop.

'Found anything?'

He turned the computer so she could see the screen. 'Nothing yet, except that these sick bastards were into porn in a big way.' His phone buzzed and vibrated. Answering, 'Williams,' he put the phone on speaker.

'Sit rep.'

'Right, Ben. Wolf was followed from the airport. The guy tailed us for a while, and then we traced him to a house in Enoggera. When we entered the property, we were confronted by four assailants. We neutralised the two who were armed and started interrogating the others when we were interrupted by the locals. All we got out of 'em was that the hostages were being taken north by boat. How far north is anyone's guess.'

'Any other intel?'

'We retrieved a laptop from the nest but it looks clean.'

'Hang onto it,' Ben barked. 'Sounds like your intel is correct. I've had a call from Salty, our contact in Port Douglas, with a lead. He said a trawler fitting the description came in during the early hours of the morning and made its way down Packers Creek. I've diverted Bugs to Cairns.' Ben's voice faded briefly as he glanced down at his watch. 'He'll be landing there shortly and should be in Port Douglas in a couple of hours. I want the three of you at the RAAF base in Amberley. If Salty's lead checks out, I need you ready to go. Report to Wing Commander Andrew Robson on the base, he'll get you kitted out and squared away.'

'Copy that. On our way.' Spooky tapped the call end button and looked over at Modeen. 'Amberley airbase. Know how to get there?'

'Yep.' Modeen released the handbrake, stomped on the accelerator, and headed toward Ashgrove and the Warrego Highway.

CHAPTER SEVEN

Bugs arrived at Cairns international airport and flicked his driver's licence onto the counter of the hire car booth.

'Yes, Mr Peterson,' the attendant said, 'any preference for type of car?'

'4WD wagon.' It had been a tiring thirty-six hour flight from Kabul in Afghanistan, and Bugs was in no mood for small talk.

The humidity engulfed him like a damp, warm blanket when he stepped out of the air-conditioned terminal, making his jeans and tee shirt feel like a heavy woollen overcoat. Dropping his duffel to the ground at his feet, he raked fingers through his military cut blonde hair and then raised his muscular arms and stretched.

It felt good to be back in Australia. While it was the country of his birth, his visits had lately been sporadic, making it feel less like home and more like a pleasant holiday destination.

Lowering his arms, he glanced at the long line of taxis to his right. When a white 4WD skirted around them and pulled up in front of him, he bent and picked up his duffel as a young attendant jumped out of the driver's side.

When Bugs handed him the rental car docket, the young man said, 'Once you've had a look over the vehicle, could you sign here, please? I've marked the few minor scratches on it that I found, but feel free to add any others you see.' He held out a pen, and a pad with 'damage report' across the top.

At six foot two, Bugs towered over the attendant. Reaching for the pen and pad, he signed the form without speaking.

'Um ... don't you want to check the car first?' The young guy sounded disappointed.

Bugs exhaled and fixed him with a measured glance. 'If it's wrong, I'll come looking for you.' He leaned closer and threw him a narrow-eyed, toothy smile. 'I know where you work.'

'Oh ... right ... OK, sir.' The attendant's eyes widened and his youthful voice wavered nervously as he backed away.

Opening the rear door, Bugs threw his bag into the back and then went to the front of the vehicle and jumped into the driver's seat. He adjusted the seat back as far as it would go and then entered 'Port

Douglas' into the on-board GPS. After checking his rear view mirror, he pulled away from the curb with a squeal of tyres.

Navigating through a maze of roundabouts, he drove along Airport Avenue and turned right onto Captain Cook Highway. The road snaked through the northern suburbs of Cairns and then hugged the coast all the way to Port Douglas. Arriving there just under an hour later, Bugs parked in the main street in front of the rustic Iron Bar Hotel.

Turning off the motor, he picked up his NatSec mobile and dialled Ben. 'Just arrived in Port Douglas. Where do I find this guy Salty?'

'He said he'd meet you at the jetty on Dixie Street at sixteen thirty, and take you to check out the trawler. Oh, and Bugs….'

'What?'

'Salty's a retired ASIO field officer, real name Richard Salt. He's in his late sixties, but don't let his age fool you. Salty's still a handy man to have around if you get into trouble. So cut him some slack, OK?'

'Whatever you say, boss.' Bugs ended the call and looked at his watch.

Good, just enough time to grab a quick bite to eat.

Bugs leaned back in the booth and swept a glance over the rustic décor of the Iron Bar Hotel. The distressed timber interior and corrugated iron with its patina of rust, gave the establishment a certain charm, he decided, and the overhead fans brought some relief from the humidity. He drained his beer glass and trekked back to the 4WD. From there it was a short drive to Dixie Street, where he parked under a tree near the jetty, rolled down his window, and waited.

It was sixteen seventeen.

His eyelids were getting heavy, and he was starting to wish he hadn't eaten such a big meal, when an old man rode past on a three wheeler bicycle, a large white esky in tow. He wore an old pair of knee-length white cotton shorts and a brightly-coloured Hawaiian shirt, unbuttoned and flapping around him. Both sides of the esky bore the words 'Salty Dick's Chowder' in bold letters, beside a fish and crab insignia.

Bugs cringed as he watched the chowder vendor park his trike in front of the 4WD and set up an umbrella. His darkly-bronzed head was bald, but he sported an impressive silver beard and a matching mass of curly hair that ran down the centre of his chest to his belly. The man's tan was so intense it made his skin look like old burnt leather.

Watching him, Bugs thought sourly, *this dude is just one big, walking melanoma.*

The old man started chanting, 'Chowder, chowder … come 'n get ya chowder … seafood chowder.' He looked over at Bugs pointedly. 'Chowder, chowder … come 'n get ya chowder … Salty Dick's chowder.'

When a couple of fisherman on the jetty put down

their rods and hurried over to the chowder wagon, the old man ladled generous scoops of a chunky white mixture into foam takeaway cups. Taking their money, he handed the fishermen a plastic spoon each along with the cups of chowder.

Glancing over at Bugs again, he caught his eye and resumed chanting. 'Chowder, chowder … come 'n get ya chowder … SALTY DICK'S chowder.' He tapped a hand on the side of the esky.

Bugs met his gaze, shook his head in a 'no thanks' gesture, and rolled up his window as another patron approached the old man and received a ladle of chowder and a spoon. This time when his customer left, greedily spooning chowder into his mouth as he went, the man walked over to stand by Bugs' window.

'Chowder, chowder …' he chanted, '… *Richard Salt's* chowder.'

The penny dropped. Bugs rolled his eyes and buzzed down his window.

Salty raised a hairy silver eyebrow and drawled, 'Not too sharp are we, son?'

'Sharp enough for you, old man,' Bugs bit back. 'And I still don't want any of your chowder.'

Salty shrugged. 'Your loss.' He glanced into the back of the 4WD. 'Grab your duffel and follow me.' Turning, he saw more patrons making their way toward his trailer and added, 'When I've finished serving these customers, that is.' Hearing Bugs give an irritated click of his tongue, he threw him a mocking smile. 'Gotta look after my clientele, got m'reputation to think about.'

Finished serving the last of his satisfied customers, Salty folded his umbrella and got back onto his trike. With a snort and a shake of his head, Bugs started the 4WD and followed as Salty pedalled over to a tree near the boat ramp. Dismounting, Salty padlocked the esky and bent to wrap a chain through the frame of the trike and around the tree.

'Who'd wanna steal that pile of junk?' Bugs strode up with his duffel over his shoulder.

Without looking at him, Salty said, 'You'd be surprised what people will do for good chowder.' He straightened and began heading down a sandy track near the boat ramp, throwing, 'You comin'?' over his shoulder.

With a resigned sigh, Bugs followed him to where a four metre aluminium dinghy rested on the beach, its anchor buried deep in the sand.

'Y'wearin' that?' Salty peered doubtfully at Bugs' clothes.

He glanced down at his white tee shirt and jeans and muttered, 'Yeah, why?'

In reply Salty merely raised his eyebrows and barked, 'Well, get in then. 'N ya might wanna spray yourself with that stuff,' and he indicated a can of tropical strength insect repellent jammed into a small shelf at the nose of the boat.

Bugs leapt into the front of the dinghy and placed

his duffel by his side while Salty pushed them off the beach. He jumped on as the dinghy began to float, skirted around Bugs and gave a yank on the pull cord. The forty horsepower outboard motor sprang into life and Salty steered them along Dickson Inlet and down Packers Creek.

Throwing Bugs a broad-brimmed straw hat that had seen better days, he said, 'At least put this on. That haircut alone's enough t'scare the natives. I had ya pegged the moment y'stepped outta the Iron Bar, 'n I'm not the only one on the lookout for agent types.'

Bugs scowled and shoved the hat onto his head as he reached for his duffel. He kept his voice low when he asked, 'When did the trawler come in?'

Salty kept his gaze forward. 'Snuck in early this mornin' when I was out fishin' for some fresh catch for m'chowder. Nearly ran right over the top of me, they did. Came in slow, hardly any lights on. That's why I noticed 'em. The trawlers usually make somethin' of an entrance, lit up like Christmas trees, most of 'em.'

'Could you tell how many were on board?'

'Nah, too dark. 'N I was too busy tryin' to get out of their way to do a head count. But reckon there's gotta be at least three of 'em.'

Bugs pulled a black tee shirt out of his duffel. Taking off the white one, he used it to mop the film of sweat off his face, muttering, 'Man, it's sticky here.' Slipping the black shirt over his taut physique, he looked at Salty. 'This better?'

Salty flicked him a glance. 'At least you won't stand out when it gets dark. 'N of course it's humid here. They don't call it the wet tropics for nothin'.'

They motored down the winding creek which to Bugs was more like a river. As with all tropical water courses, the time of year and the ebb and flow of the tides combined to make a big impact on the saltwater creek's depth and breadth.

Salty slowed the boat and let it drift, the water slapping greasily against the aluminium hull, while he rummaged around in a large blue plastic container under the rear seat. He extracted a fish head and tied it to the centre of a circular crab net. Pulling out his mobile phone, he marked the spot on the phone's GPS app, and then threw the crab net over the side.

'Really?' Bugs looked at him sharply. 'You're crab fishing *now?*'

Salty gave a resigned sigh and shook his head at the younger man. 'Well, we don't want to draw any unnecessary attention now do we, son? I'm always down here puttin' out m'nets, so people are used to seein' me here.' Turning to twist the throttle on the outboard, Salty motored up the creek another twenty metres, and then slowed and threw out another net. Bending as though to get something from off the floor, he said quietly, 'Comin' up on your right.'

Bugs immediately leaned back against the dinghy's bow and pulled the brim of the hat down over his eyes. Crossing his arms over his chest and resting his feet on the gunwale, he presented a picture of water-borne relaxation. As they motored past a branch in the creek, a blue-hulled trawler came into view. It was moored against a weathered wooden jetty. An olive-skinned man stood at the stern dressed in black trousers and matching long-sleeved shirt. He stared at them as they puttered unconcernedly past.

Salty slowed and threw out another net, then moved on another twenty metres and did it again. Without looking at Bugs, he said, 'That the trawler you're lookin' for?'

Bugs stayed in the same pose. 'Certainly fits the description, and the guy standing on the deck doesn't look much like a fisherman to me.' Reaching up an arm, he lifted the hat's brim with one finger and shot Salty a meaningful glance. 'My guess is the hostages aren't on board, otherwise there'd be more than one guard.'

'Hostages?' Salty fixed him with a steely-eyed gaze.

Realising he's said more than he should've, Bugs ignored the question, instead asking his own. 'Do you know where that trail leads to, the one from the jetty?'

'Yeah, to a house on the other side of those mangroves.' Salty squinted at him. 'How many hostages?'

Bugs paused before deciding he'd may as well come clean, the cat was already out of the bag. 'Three males. Two are overseas diplomats.' He swiftly changed the subject. 'So, is that house easily accessible from the road?'

'Nah, it's set well back from Lakeland Ave. There's a dirt track off Lakeland that leads straight to it, but access from the track is difficult. The property backs onto the water and is surrounded by an impressive security fence, with heavy wrought iron gates. The place is owned by some rich guy ... Akeem Jibril, I think his name is. But I've never met the man.'

'Right,' Bugs snapped. 'I need to get a close look at the house. Can you pull up on the other side of the tributary branch? I'll try to get at it through the mangroves.'

Salty raised an eyebrow at him. 'Y'know there's crocs, snakes and all sorts of nasty things livin' in there, don't ya?'

'I have to give it a try. It's my best chance to get a look at the house without being seen, isn't it?'

'Guess so ... they sure wouldn't be expectin' anyone t'crawl through the mangroves to visit 'em.' Salty steered the boat back past the trawler and stopped fifty metres up from it, in the main stream next to the mangroves. He pointed a gnarled finger through the thick watery growth of trees. 'The house should be about a hundred metres through there.' He glanced at Bugs. 'Y'got a weapon?'

'Nah.' Bugs had grabbed hold of a branch and was about to exit the dinghy. 'Airport security get twitchy when I try to bring my matching pair of fifty cal Desert

Eagles into the country.' He took off the hat and threw it toward Salty. 'And this won't be much help in there, I wouldn't think.'

'Hang on.' Salty tossed the hat onto the seat and then rummaged in the blue container. Pulling out a sealed plastic bag covered in fish guts, he broke the seal and took out something wrapped in an old rag. Handing it to Bugs, he said gruffly, 'It aint a Desert Eagle, but it's better than usin' harsh language on 'em.'

Bugs unwrapped the rag to reveal a Glock seventeen. 'Nice, Salty. Thanks mate.' Pulling back the slide, he checked the breach. Satisfied it was clear and the clip was full, he wedged the barrel down the back of his pants and slipped over the side into the brackish, knee-deep water.

And disappeared into the mangroves.

CHAPTER EIGHT

Night was falling in Port Douglas when Bugs emerged. He waded out of the deepening shadow of the mangroves and glanced up to where Salty's dinghy sat ten metres away. It bobbed gently on the water right where he'd left it, the glow of a small hurricane lamp gilding the water around it. He heard faint strains of music from a radio, and saw Salty in the lamplight. The old man was lying back with his ankles crossed on the gunwale, hands behind his head, and hat over his face.

'Hey Salty, over here.'

At the sound of the hushed call, Salty snapped upright. Catching sight of Bugs, he grabbed a paddle and pushed his way along the mangroves toward him. When Bugs grabbed the nose of the dinghy, Salty moved to the back to counterbalance the little boat while he climbed aboard.

'So how'd you get on, youngster?'

Bugs slumped onto the metal bench seat with a grunt, seawater dripping off the bottoms of his jeans. 'Found it.' He nodded. 'Plenty of armed guards patrolling the house, a couple of 4WD wagons and a Bedford van parked out back. But I didn't see any sign of hostages.' He ran a hand over his hair. 'I'll have to report in, Ben'll be sweatin' on a sit rep.'

'Not a problem.' Salty peered at him and then reached forward to pluck a leech off the side of Bugs' neck. He held it up. The blood-engorged parasite squirmed in his fingers.

Bugs looked at Salty sideways, gave a lopsided grin and said drily, 'That's not goin' in the chowder is it?'

Smirking, Salty flicked the blood-sucking invertebrate into the trees. 'Right then, I'll take us down the creek a bit further and we'll check the crab pots.' He pushed the dinghy away from the mangroves and yanked on the outboard motor's cord. The engine started on the first pull and he steered them down to where they'd positioned the first pot.

While Salty busied himself pulling up his hall of crustaceans, Bugs took out his mobile and dialled Ben. His call was answered promptly and he began rapping out his report, taking care to keep his voice low, knowing listening ears often hide in the unlikeliest of places.

'Yep. Positive ID on the trawler. It's moored down Packers Creek, at a residence off Lakeland Avenue.

Salty tells me the place is owned by one Akeem Jibril.' As he said the name, he glanced at Salty, who nodded confirmation.

Bugs continued with his report. 'I counted five guards around the house and one on the trawler. The guys at the house are armed with M4s.' He paused briefly to listen and then said, 'There are two 4WD wagons and a Bedford van parked out the back of the property. No sighting of the hostages so I can't confirm they're located there, but I'd reckon it's our best bet. All was quiet on the trawler and the guard looked pretty casual, so I doubt the prisoners are still on board.' He listened again.

'I'm on the creek with Salty, not far from where the trawler's moored.' Having completed his sit rep, Bugs paused and then said, 'Yes Sir,' and ended the call. He turned to Salty. 'How many times a night do you normally check your crab pots?'

'Twice,' Salty said, keeping his gaze on the water ahead, checking for submerged flotsam. 'Due to check 'em now and again in about three hours.'

'Perfect.' Bugs' expression lightened and he threw Salty a wink.

Ben rose to his feet as operations manager Jack Pender entered the briefing room in NatSec's Melbourne office.

Returning Ben's nod of greeting, Jack announced,

'Well, we've managed to piss off the Feds, MI6 and the CIA with our recent activities.' He dropped a bulging folder onto the table and looked at Ben, adding with a wry grin, 'Good to see we're leading the charge.'

Ben gave an amused snort as Jack pulled out a chair at the head of the table. Both men took their seats and Jack opened the folder and gazed down at its contents.

'The Feds have interviewed the two men they picked up in Enoggera.' He raised his eyes to glance at Ben. 'Apparently your team "busted up the place and the blokes real good".'

Ben shrugged a broad shoulder. 'Just doing their job.'

Returning his gaze to the folder, Jack gave a swift nod of agreement. 'The CIA and MI6 agents will be down here shortly, along with Feds chief Sullivan, and Ross and Paul from ASIS. Harper's escorting them through security.' He looked up. 'We'll wait for them to arrive before starting the meeting proper.' Pausing to rest his arms on the table, he eyed Ben. 'But where are we up to now?'

Taking his cue from Jack, Ben kept his tone low. 'Agent Peterson has verified that the trawler is in Port Douglas, moored outside a private residence on Packers Creek. He believes the hostages have been moved into the heavily guarded house.'

Jack nodded without speaking as Ben continued. 'Pine Gap hooked me up with the thermal imaging satellite and after doing a sweep of the place, I concur with Peterson's intel. There appears to be three persons huddled together in one of the central rooms, indicative of the hostages. I also picked up the heat signatures of three individuals roaming about inside, probably guards.'

Jack nodded again. 'Your next move?'

'I've got a Globemaster on standby and my team prepped in Amberley.'

Jack raised a hand. 'Ben, considering the contentious nature of this mission, I want you on the ground, leading it.'

'I thought you might, Jack, so I planned to coordinate the operation in person. As soon as this meeting's over, I'm on the Globemaster and heading to Amberley to join the team.' Ben fell silent as five men entered the room, accompanied by Harper.

The two men rose and Jack said, 'Welcome gentlemen, please be seated. Thank you, Harper, that will be all.' He resumed his seat at the head of the U-shaped table and gestured toward Ben while addressing the new arrivals. 'This is Ben Smith, NatSec Team Leader. Ben, this is …,' and he indicated each person as he went, '… Brian Koller CIA, Alan McIntosh MI6, and of course you know Ross Wentworth ASIS, Paul Edwards Navy, and Federal Police Chief Warwick Sullivan.'

The men exchanged nods as Jack sat forward and said briskly, 'Right. Let's make this brief, shall we?'

Before anyone else could respond, a scowling Warwick Sullivan thumped the table with a fist. 'Look,' he barked, 'we've got the ball when it comes to security for the G20 summit, and we need to be kept informed at all times.' He pointed an accusing finger toward Jack and Ben. 'We can't have your people running around killing everyone and destroying valuable evidence.'

Jack regarded him for a moment before saying solemnly, 'We're sorry for the loss of your young agent, Chief. But you can't blame NatSec for your current woes. It appears you dropped the ball well before we were engaged to assist.'

Sullivan's face flushed and he opened his mouth to argue but was cut off by a raised hand from Jack. 'We're committed to keeping you *all* informed,' Jack said in a deep, authoritative voice, 'as new intel comes to light.' Lowering his hand, he swept a glance around the table. 'However, as you know only too well, in gathering that intel our agents must adapt and respond to each situation they encounter. If they hesitate to act for whatever reason they can not only endanger their own lives, but also jeopardise attempts to rescue the hostages ... alive ... which is something we *all* want and are striving to achieve. I trust you will keep that in mind.'

There was a ripple of movement, a nodding of heads and some deep breaths taken around the table as Jack went on. 'And on the subject of information, I'd like to mention that we haven't received any intel from you.' He fixed Sullivan with a steely gaze. 'Chief, I assume you've interrogated the men our agents tracked down and subdued in Brisbane?'

Sullivan gave a surly nod.

'So, can you tell us what you've learnt from these interrogations?'

The Federal Police chief sucked in a breath and then exhaled loudly. 'We haven't been able to extract any other information about the trawler, only that it was headed somewhere north of Brisbane which we … you … already knew.' He frowned. 'That was all we got from them,' adding churlishly, 'But then *we* don't go around breaking peoples' legs for information.'

Ignoring the last comment, Jack said coolly, 'So our intel was helpful.'

Sullivan threw him a narrow-eyed glance and said reluctantly, 'Well … at least we know what we're looking for.'

'Yes.' Jack eyed the officers and agents sitting down the table from him. Wentworth and Edwards gazed back at him calmly, while the CIA's Koller slouched rather than sat in his chair. He wore a suitcase-rumpled polo shirt and jeans and was chewing gum with an open mouth. MI6's agent McIntosh, on the other hand, sat straight-backed and attentive in his crisp grey suit, white shirt and silver-grey tie.

Jack looked at each of them in turn. 'Have the other agencies anything new to share?'

Wentworth, Edwards and Koller all shook their heads without speaking, while McIntosh said in precise Oxford English, 'Only that we're ramping up our presence here to protect our other delegates.'

Jack rubbed his chin and sighed. 'Right. Well, to the best of our knowledge, two days ago the hostages were on a trawler heading somewhere north of Brisbane. As that's our only lead at this point, I suggest we get to it and find that trawler.' He shoved some loose pieces of paperwork back into the folder in front of him and snapped it shut. Rising to his feet, he nodded to the other six. 'Thank you for your attendance gentlemen, that's all for now.' With a final, dismissive nod to the others, Jack turned and left the briefing room.

As Ben went to follow him, Koller put a hand on his arm and drawled, 'Just a minute.'

Ben stopped and eyed the other man from his impressive height. Koller immediately released his arm and said more congenially, 'I mean, do you have a minute?'

'One minute. What is it?'

'I just need to tell you the same thing I told him,' and he inclined his head at a still seated Sullivan.

'Which is?' Ben glanced pointedly at his watch.

'That the US doesn't view kindly the kidnapping of its VIPs in other countries, *especially* when those countries assured us they would keep our people safe.'

'Come now, Koller, old chum.' McIntosh had sauntered up to join them. 'The US isn't alone in this. Don't forget there's a Brit and an Aussie caught up in it too. And you know as well as I do it's impossible to protect everyone everywhere from everything.' He threw Ben an empathetic half smile.

'I'm glad you acknowledge that.' Ben narrowed his eyes, and when he spoke, his tone brooked no argument. 'And here's another fact you need to keep in mind. NatSec was called in *after* the event, and so far we've uncovered all the intel there is on the case.'

At the intensity in Ben's voice and gaze, Koller took a step back. 'And of course we're grateful for that, but you need to understand something. We believe the terrorists only took the other two hostages as an added incentive.'

Widening his eyes, McIntosh mused aloud, 'So that England and Australia would pressure the US to concede to the kidnapper's demands.' He nodded. 'Makes sense.'

'Yes it does.' It was obvious this was not news to Ben. Growling, 'And now, if that's all, we need to get to work, and fast,' he dipped his head, and on receiving nods from Koller and McIntosh, marched from the room.

Striding down the corridor, Ben stopped at the doorway of NatSec's Senior Computer Tech's office. He was pleased to see James O'Neill at his desk. 'James!' he barked, 'you doing anything for the next six hours?'

Looking up, James gave a doubtful smile. 'Well, I

had planned on heading home and having dinner with the wife and kids.'

'Call and tell them you have to work back. I need you on a priority job. Be ready to go in fifteen minutes, I'll meet you in the carpark.'

'Priority job? What—'

'A confiscated laptop we need checked out for intel.'

'Laptop?' James frowned and rose to his feet. 'Mac or Windows-based?'

'Could be either.' Ben was already leaving. 'Just grab your bag of tricks and be ready to go in fifteen.'

James stood scratching his head for a brief moment as Harper went past the doorway, ushering the murmuring guests from the briefing room and escorting them out of the building.

Ben made a few other calls and then stuck his head into the Operations Manager's office on his way past. 'I'm off, Jack. Thanks for keeping the meeting short.'

Glancing up from his paperwork, Jack fixed Ben with a steady gaze. 'Well, we couldn't have it turning into a talk-fest or a slanging match, that would've achieved nothing except an unnecessary delay.' Pausing, he sat back, took off his reading glasses and added quietly, 'Good luck, Ben.'

• • •

As instructed, James was waiting by Ben's Aurion. The men were loading up the car as Harper hurried over to join them.

Ben threw her the car keys. 'Airport, thanks Harper.'

She gave him a broad smile. 'Airport shuttle, at your service. Qantas, Virgin or Jetstar?'

'Neither. We need you to drop us at the freight terminal.'

'Freight terminal, copy that.'

Harper skilfully negotiated the heavy city traffic and dropped Ben and James at the terminal a short time later. After grabbing his duffel from the Aurion's boot and handing James his bag, Ben led the way with a long-legged stride to a freight counter at the end of the building. Two RAAF officers greeted them and proceeded to escort them onto the tarmac toward a waiting C-17 Globemaster.

James' jaw dropped and he stopped mid-stride, gazing open-mouthed and wide-eyed at the massive cargo plane poised on the runway apron. Realising he'd stopped, Ben turned to him with a puzzled frown.

James stuttered, 'W-where the hell is this laptop?'

Ben grabbed him by an arm and continued walking toward the military jet. 'Relax, James. The computer's at Amberley, we'll pick it up from there and then head north. While we're travelling, I want you to check it out for hidden files or other pertinent info that might help with the mission.'

'OK.' James still looked doubtful.

'You're just doing the round trip,' Ben said amiably. 'The RAAF guys will drop you back here after we've made the jump. So make the most of the ride, it's not every day a civilian gets to fly in a Globemaster.'

'Right, so just making sure … I'm not expected to jump?'

'Of course not.' Ben chuckled and slapped James on his visibly relaxing shoulder. 'We wouldn't do that to you, buddy.'

CHAPTER NINE

Ben and James walked up the rear ramp of the Globemaster as its four huge PW2000 Pratt and Whitney jet engines whined into life. The gigantic cargo hold was empty except for a cluster of ten seats up front, behind the cockpit. Their footsteps echoed along the bare metal floor as they made their way to the front of the plane. James gave a drawn-out whistle as he gazed around, taking in the sheer size of the plane's interior with its exposed fuselage bracing and metal walls hung with cargo netting.

Ben pointed to one of the seats. 'Sit down and strap in.' Continuing on to the cockpit, he opened the door and stuck his head in to talk to the RAAF pilots, before taking a seat beside James and strapping himself in.

Ten minutes later they were thundering down the runway, and within moments the combined one hundred and sixty thousand pound thrust of the four turbofan engines lifted the essentially empty grey leviathan effortlessly skyward.

'Must be some laptop,' an awed James said as he turned in his seat and looked down the cavernous fuselage of the cargo plane. 'Isn't this a bit over the top for a ride to Amberley?'

'We're only stopping at Amberley to pick up the troops and the laptop. After that we're flying on to Port Douglas.'

'Right.'

Ben fixed him with a level gaze. 'Like I said, I need you to check the laptop for hidden files, any intel that might help us identify terrorist strongholds or assets.'

James regarded him seriously. 'How will I know what I'm looking for?'

'Luke Williams has already cracked the password and done a basic search, but I need you to go over it in case he's missed something. You'll be looking for any reference to the hostages, or a guy by the name of Akeem Jibril … pretty much anything that doesn't smell right.' Ben pulled a folded piece of paper from his top pocket and handed it to James. 'Also look for any reference to this trawler.'

James took the paper and unfolded it. It was a copy of the photo Wolf had taken at Scarborough Marina. He nodded. 'Not a problem.'

Ben took out his mobile from a back pocket, thumbed a number and placed the phone next to his ear. 'JD,' he barked when the call was answered, 'I'm on my way up from Melbourne on a Globe, ETA just under two hours.'

'Roger. Do you have any further intel?'

'I'll brief you in the air. Bring four HALO chutes, and I need you guys armed and ready for night ops.'

Salty turned the knob of the hurricane lamp to the full-on position and held it forward as he puttered the dinghy back down Packers Creek, checking his crab nets as he went. When he'd retrieved four large mud crabs from the five strategically placed nets, he turned to Bugs with a pleased grin.

'Check out these babies,' and he held up a large black crab bound with string to keep its powerful pincers in check. When he saw Bugs looking at the string, he said, 'Gotta watch those big claws, they can snip off a man's finger or toe real easy if he's not careful.'

Bugs gave a low whistle as Salty went on jauntily, 'All big 'uns tonight, I'm doin' well.' He threw the crab into the bucket with the others and sat beside the outboard again. 'Right, we'll take these home and come back later. Sound OK to you?'

'Fine. Just as long as I'm back here in about three and a half to four hours for when the others "drop in".' Flashing Salty one of his trademark toothy grins, Bugs reached down and picked up a rag from the floor of the dinghy. Pulling the Glock from the back of his pants, he started wrapping it in the cloth.

Salty held up a hand to stop him. 'Keep it. Until this is over.'

Looking down at the pistol, Bugs raised and lowered his hand, feeling the weight of the weapon. 'Thanks again Salty, cheers mate.' He shoved the gun down the front of his jeans until the pistol grip was just visible above the waistband.

Watching him, Salty enquired, 'So, whatcha wanna do in the meantime?'

'Well, I could do with a clean-up. And I need to organise a coupl'a things.'

'What kinda things?'

Bugs counted them off on his fingers. 'A mask, fins, a signal light and a waterproof pack.'

'That won't be a problem, I know just where to get 'em.' Salty grabbed hold of the outboard motor's throttle, but then paused and glanced at Bugs. 'Say, what happens if they, the ones at the house, decide to bug out in the meantime?'

'Don't worry,' and Bugs threw him a wink, 'I've got that covered.'

Salty gave a lopsided grin and snorted, 'I bet you do,' as he twisted the throttle. The dinghy's bow lifted as the propeller dug into the water and powered the little boat forward.

———

Modeen walked back to where Spooky and Wolf sat in the huge mess hall at Amberley airbase. They looked up expectantly as she thrust her mobile back into a pocket.

'We're up in two hours. Ben wants us ready for night ops.'

Spooky sat back and stared at her. 'Sounds like Bugs' intel at Port Douglas might've checked out.'

Modeen nodded. 'Ben's flying up from Melbourne in a Globe. He wants four HALO chutes prepped and ready.'

'Right.' Spooky got to his feet. 'I'll go chase up Wing Commander Robson and make the arrangements. Meet you back here in half an hour.' He strode out of the mess hall leaving the other two alone.

In the silence that followed Spooky's departure, Wolf's voice sounded deeper than usual when he said to Modeen, 'How you holdin' up?' He gazed at her with concern in his dark eyes.

She stared down at her hands and mumbled, 'I'll be OK once we've got Dad back safe and sound.'

Wolf shuffled closer, put his arm around her and gave her a squeeze. 'Don't worry, we'll get him back in one piece … Mrs Ryan.' He grinned wryly at her.

She gave him a wan smile in return, leaned her head on his broad shoulder and murmured, 'I'm glad we're all back together on this one.'

He pulled her closer and rested his stubbled chin on her hair, breathing in her warm, womanly scent. After a brief moment he murmured thoughtfully, 'Four chutes. Looks like the big fella's comin' out from behind his desk and joining us on the drop, so the intel must be pretty accurate.'

'Yep, sounds promising.' Modeen lifted her head and straightened in her seat. 'You up for another coffee?' At Wolf's nod, she rose and made her way to the self-serve urn simmering away in the corner.

A short time later Spooky returned as promised. Announcing, 'All sorted, follow me,' he led them back to the carpark and the waiting Aurion. Pointing to the northern side of the base, he said, 'Drive in through those boom gates and over to that hangar.' At the boom gates, he flashed the security pass Robson had given him and the heavy boom lifted. 'Just drive straight into the hangar and park in the far corner.'

As Modeen nosed the car into the hangar and parked it, a small baggage handling vehicle towing a trailer pulled up next to them. On the trailer sat four camouflage backpacks, four HALO chutes, and two padded weapons cases. The three agents exited the Aurion and wasted no time helping the baggage handler remove the gear from the trailer and stack it next to the car. When they'd finished, the handler gave them a nod and took off across the tarmac.

Walking to stand in the open hangar doorway, they took in the size of the well-lit base. Three huge grey Globemaster C-17s sat to their left, dwarfing a nearby de Havilland Caribou. On their far right an F/A-18F Super Hornet was being towed into its hangar.

'Well, I guess it's hurry up-n-wait time.' Wolf raised his arms and stretched. After a short pause he muttered, 'Gettin' cool out here.' The night air had started to roll in. Turning, he said over his shoulder, 'I'm gonna try and get some shut eye,' and strolled back inside the hangar. As he lowered his six foot one frame onto the floor next to the backpacks, Modeen glanced at Spooky.

'Doesn't sound like a bad idea.'

'Got me.' Spooky set the alarm on his watch. 'We might be lucky and get in an hour and a half before Ben arrives.'

An hour later, Modeen nudged them both with the toe of her boot. They awoke to see her standing over them, holding three styrofoam cups of coffee on a cardboard tray. 'They've made good time,' she announced, 'and will be here in twenty minutes.' She bent to hand them each a steaming cup as they sat up and stretched.

Reaching over to slap a yawning Spooky on the back, Wolf said, 'Nothin' like sleepin' on a cold cement floor with your backpack as a pillow.'

'Yeah,' Spooky replied drily, taking the cup from Modeen. 'Beats sleeping suspended in a swamp any day of the week.' He took a grateful swig of coffee. 'Anyway, I guess we'd better get our kit sorted.'

They stripped down the backpacks and opened one of the weapon cases. Gazing down at the two M4 carbines, Wolf grabbed one, pulled back the slide, checked the breach and then released it. 'We need to put Robson on the shit list,' he muttered darkly.

'Why?' Spooky said.

'These M4s have seen more action than your mother.' His face worked as he tried to swallow a grin.

Spooky growled, 'You leave my mother outta this, that woman's a saint.' At Wolf's bark of laughter, he chuckled and they bumped fists.

Modeen was only half listening. It was an old joke between them, one she'd heard many times before. She opened the other weapons case and examined one of the M4s. With a shake of her head, she replaced the rifle and rose. Moving to the back of the Aurion, she opened the boot and pulled out an MP5. She attached the silencer and laid it next to her kit, then got busy filling its clip with nine millimetre ammo.

Twenty minutes later the three of them were standing in front of the hangar wearing their backpacks and with their chutes by their sides. They were staring out at the brightly lit runway as a Globemaster made its lumbering approach. The pilots guided it to a smooth touch-down, the enormous wheels of the triple tandem undercarriage cushioning the fifty-three metre aircraft's arrival on the tarmac.

They watched as it taxied down the runway toward them and then turned. It came to a rolling stop, its huge tail wing towering over them. As the four engines whirred to an idle, the plane's rear ramp lowered and they saw Ben standing at the top of it. He waved them on and they jogged toward the loading ramp. As they went past him into the cargo hold, Spooky dropped a HALO chute at Ben's feet, and Wolf did the same with a backpack.

Collecting the gear, Ben followed them inside.

Moments later, the ramp lifted and locked back into place, and the whine of the four jet engines became a surge of power as the Globemaster taxied back out onto the runway.

CHAPTER TEN

Bugs followed behind Salty in the rented 4WD as he led the way to his place high on the hill behind the main street. Watching Salty's tanned, stringy legs pumping the pedals as he negotiated the hill, Bugs found himself thinking, *scooting around on that trike must keep the old man pretty fit.*

Salty was starting to slow as they crested the top of the steep hill, but then took a sharp turn into a tree covered driveway. Bugs nosed the 4WD in behind him and parked in the drive, in front of what had looked, from the road verge, like a tiny red cedar cottage. When he got out and made his way toward the house, he could see it had two levels with the lower one built into the side of the hill. The top floor had an expansive back deck looking over the rise and toward the inlet, while the smaller lower deck sported a jacuzzi.

Salty parked his bike in the carport and took the

chowder esky and crab bucket from off the back. Carrying them up the stairs, he tilted his head at Bugs. 'C'mon in, youngster, make yourself at home.'

Once inside, he headed for the kitchen and dumped the containers on the floor. After rummaging around in the cupboards he pulled out a large pot, half filled it with water, and threw in some salt. Placing the pot on the biggest gas burner on the island bench, he got the flame going beneath it and then dropped a lid on the pot with a satisfied nod.

He went to join Bugs and found him standing in the lounge, gazing at the timber that lined the ceiling and walls of the room. 'That there's Sequoia on the ceiling and Oregon Pine on the walls,' he said proudly.

'This is a beaut place.' Bugs threw him a smile. 'And a great view off your deck.'

'Been to check it out already, have ya?' Salty went over to the glass doors leading to the deck and gazed out. 'Yep, that view was what sold me on this place. A man likes being able to look down on the rest of the world sometimes, know what I'm sayin'?'

'Distance yourself from it all, you mean?'

Salty nodded. 'Knew you'd understand.' His expression hardened. 'That's a downside to this business we … that is you … are in. You get to see the seedy side of the world in all its ugliness. Still…' and he slapped his hands together, 'a man's gotta do what a man's gotta do. Right, now follow me, youngster.'

He led the way down a steep flight of hardwood

stairs and stopped in the corridor near the lined stair-well. Throwing Bugs a wink, he put a finger against the side of one of the steps at eye level and pushed. The step moved an inch into the wall and a door-sized panel under the stairwell clunked open. Stepping inside, Salty flicked on a light switch.

Bugs followed him in and swept a glance around the three by two metre room. His jaw dropped when he saw what was hanging in pride of place on the end wall. A pristine pair of gold, limited edition fifty calibre Desert Eagle pistols, complete with pearl handles, glinted in the glow of the overhead light. When he could tear his eyes away from the gleaming pistols, he noticed hanging beneath them two Smith and Wesson revolvers, one fifty calibre and the other a forty-four magnum. Beneath them again were four Glock nine-teens. And underneath the handguns sat a rack of assault and sniper rifles.

Realising he'd been standing staring open-mouthed at the impressive armoury, he licked his lips and murmured, 'I love you man,' to a grinning Salty. 'Oh yeah, this is my kinda house.'

Salty narrowed his eyes. 'Don't be gettin' any ideas about them Eagles, youngster,' adding when Bugs flicked him a guilty smirk, 'they're staying right where they are.'

With a shake of his head and a regretful snort, Bugs moved closer to examine the rifles. 'You've got a Barrett … and is that a QBU-88 sniper rifle?'

'Right both times.' Salty opened a chest on the floor to his right and pulled out a pair of fins and a mask. 'Got these from a Navy buddy of mine, should be good gear.' He handed them to Bugs and rummaged in the chest again. 'This might come in handy too.' He held out a wrist strap with an in-built compass. 'Now for that waterproof bag.' Dipping his hand back into the chest, he brought out a waterproof pack. 'This should do the job. Got tags so you can strap it to your back if y'want.' He passed it to Bugs, mumbling, 'Signal torch …,' and rubbed his chin. 'Now … where did I put that? Ah yes.' Snapping closed the lid of the chest, he reached up to grasp a torch mounted on the wall to his left. 'This should do the job. It's got a red lens cover and can't be seen by anyone not in direct line of sight.'

Bugs took the proffered torch and added it to the pile of gear he was holding. 'Thanks again, Salty.' He nodded his gratitude at the old man. 'How can I repay you?'

Salty flicked a dismissive hand at him. 'Forget it, Ben looks after me. Keeps me well supplied.' He grinned and winked at Bugs and then turned toward the doorway. 'Now, come on youngster, wipe that drool from off your mouth and let's see if we can't fill it with some fresh caught, fresh cooked mud crab. Accompanied by some of Salty Dick's famous seafood chowder, of course.'

Bugs returned the grin. 'Got me.'

They wandered back upstairs, where they heard the

pot bubbling away on the stove. Exclaiming, 'You beauty!' Salty took the lid off the pot and then reached into the bucket to pull out the two biggest crabs. 'Right, in ya go my lovelies,' and he slid them into the boiling water.

Bugs took a seat at the kitchen table and watched as his obliging host took a container of chowder from the fridge. After ladling some into a saucepan and setting it on the stove to warm, Salty began laying out plates and cutlery.

'You'll make someone a fine wife one day,' Bugs drawled, and then chuckled at Salty's unimpressed, 'Humph!'

Still laughing, Bugs offered, 'Wanna hand?'

'Nah,' Salty threw over his shoulder, 'I'm right.'

'So, how long you been outta ASIO?'

'About fifteen years now. Though, technically speakin', I wasn't with ASIO exactly. More like that NatSec you belong to.' As he spoke, Salty sliced chunks off a crusty bread loaf, using deft strokes of a very sharp knife. 'The last ten of those years I was behind a desk and didn't get out much. Guess that's why I decided to retire.' He straightened and glanced at Bugs. 'But that don't mean I'm not interested in what's goin' on in the world. For one thing, I've noticed it's gettin' a lot smaller. When I was in the game proper, most of my ops were overseas.' He went back to slicing the bread. 'Now it looks like they're bringin' the fight closer to home.'

Bugs nodded gravely without speaking.

'Right, they should be 'bout done by now.' Salty took the lid off the bubbling pot and a savoury, briny steam billowed to the ceiling. Using tongs, he lifted one of the crabs out of the water. It had changed colour from dull black to bright orange-red. 'Yep, we're ready to go.' He looked at Bugs. 'Tell ya what y'can do.'

'Yeah, what?' Bugs got to his feet.

'Grab us a beer each, they're in the fridge. And there's stubby cubbies on the counter there.'

'I'll get one for you, Salty, but I'll save mine for later.' While Bugs got the icy beer bottle from out of the fridge and slipped it into a stubby holder, Salty broke up the hot mud crabs and served them on a large platter, with side bowls of the now warm and aromatic chowder.

Putting the beer in front of Salty, Bugs hastened to take a seat. Licking his lips, he wasted no time tucking into the food. Having demolished his bowl of chowder with gratifying speed, he started into two giant mud crab claws, pausing only once to remark on the sweetness of the creamy flesh. Dropping the last bit of empty shell on his plate, he sat back and said, 'That's not half bad, Salty.'

He was interrupted by the urgent vibrations of his mobile. Sitting forward, all traces of joviality gone, he yanked the phone from his pocket and answered, 'Peterson.' He listened intently for a minute, and then nodded and said briskly, 'Right. Watch for a red signal light.' Slipping the phone back into his pocket, he looked at his watch and rapped, 'We'd better make tracks, Salty. The unit's dropping in at twenty-three fifteen, and I need to get on that trawler and be ready for their aerial assault.'

'No problem.' Salty was already on his feet and clearing the table.

Minutes later, the two men jumped in the rented 4WD and made their way down to the boat ramp. It was a dark night, and they didn't speak as they once more launched the dinghy and made their way along Packers Creek in the slight glow of the waning moon. Once seated, Bugs opened the waterproof backpack and stuffed his phone, torch and the Glock inside it.

Keeping his voice low, he asked Salty, 'Do you reckon you can get me within sixty metres of that trawler?'

'Shouldn't be a problem.'

It was approaching twenty-two fifty when Salty leaned forward and whispered, 'Coming up on your left.'

'Right. Hold up here for a second.' Bugs took off his shirt and slipped on the backpack, compass and fins. To clear the mask and prevent fogging, he spat into it and rinsed it in the water, before donning it and slipping soundlessly over the side of the dinghy.

Salty frowned and muttered, 'I told you about the crocs right?'

'Yeah yeah. Just get me within sixty metres of the trawler.'

Salty twisted the throttle and the little dinghy puttered forward with Bugs clinging to the gunwale with one hand. Whistling softly under his breath, Salty nosed the dinghy into the tributary branch of the river where the trawler was moored, and approached the other boat from the rear. When the guard at the trawler's stern shone a bright torch beam onto him, Salty immediately threw up a hand to shade his eyes, while the dinghy continued drifting closer to the other vessel.

'Hey! What are you doing?' the guard yelled.

'Oh! Sorry, took a wrong turn.' Salty chortled good-naturedly. 'Too many beers with dinner,' adding, 'Just checkin' me pots.' Waving an apologetic hand in the guard's direction, he powered the dinghy forward into a wide, slow arc. When it was safe, he glanced at the gunwale.

Bugs had gone.

Thinking, *good luck, youngster,* Salty began whistling again as he chugged up the river and away.

Bugs had taken a compass bearing and a deep breath just before Salty made the turn after having managed to drop him within forty metres of the trawler.

Thinking, *well done, old mate,* Bugs had released his hold on the dinghy and let himself slip beneath the dark water. Diving down about a metre, he swam toward the trawler. Keeping his right arm straight and extended in front of him and his other hand gripping his right elbow, he focused on the faintly illuminated pointer of the compass on his left wrist while counting fin kicks as he swam.

Estimating he was getting close to the vessel, he held his right hand palm forward, and within another five kicks touched the trawler's hull with his fingers. Taking his time, he floated upward and allowed his head to break the surface of the water, being careful not to make any noise. He glanced up at the back of the boat. As he'd hoped, it was pitch black and would provide plenty of cover. He reached up to grasp the trawler's recessed back steps when a sound above made him freeze in the water. It was the guard, talking on a two way.

His voice was guttural, his English stilted.

'No! It was just that crazy old chowder man.' He clicked the button and Bugs could just catch another voice speaking amid the radio static. Then the guard spoke again. 'Yes, yes, just checking his nets.' There was a clunk as the guard put down the radio, followed by a click and a flare, and then the aroma of cigarette smoke reached Bugs' nose.

The guard took a deep drag, exhaled the smoke upward into the balmy night air, and then stared moodily at the lit end of his cigarette. This was so boring. How much longer would he have to stay on the damned boat? Surely someone would come to relieve him soon. With a quick, irritated move of his fingers, he flicked ash off the end of his cigarette and took another drag. Tilting his head, he blew smoke into the air and listened to the sound of a plane high above. He sneered. Yet another jet no doubt carrying more ridiculous tourists to Cairns Airport....

About to put the cigarette to his lips again, he stiffened as a pair of strong hands reached from behind to grasp his head in a vicelike grip and wrench it violently to the right.

As the guard's body slumped to the floor, Bugs slipped off the backpack and quickly checked the rest of the trawler.

Clear.

Shoving the Glock down the back of his wet jeans and grabbing the torch and his phone, he positioned himself on the starboard side of the deck. Glancing at his mobile, he checked the time.

Twenty-two ten.

He paused and cocked his head, listening for a few moments. Hearing the faint drone of four jet engines high above, he flicked on the torch, raised it above his head, and began making circular motions skyward.

CHAPTER ELEVEN

A Bedford van pulled off the highway onto a well-graded gravel track and promptly turned off its headlights. Using only the glow of its parking lights, it followed the track through the sparse, scrubby clearing and rolled to a slow stop on the leaf-strewn driveway beside the derelict army Nissan hut.

The two men in the truck eyed the Triumph motorcycle parked outside the rear of the barn-like building. They exchanged a significant glance before peering through the windscreen, straining for signs of the bike's rider. No glimmer of light shone through the wire netting covering some of the shutter-like windows, and all was still outside the old corrugated iron building.

One of the men nodded to the other and grabbed a pair of bolt cutters from off the floor. They opened their doors carefully and got out of the vehicle. Making their way to the southern end of the hut, they found a sign at the base of the entranceway ramp, warning visitors to stay out of the dilapidated building for their own safety. The battered timber doors at the top of the shallow ramp were closed, but they could see a broken padlock hanging loosely from a chain looped over a door handle.

Pulling open one of the doors just wide enough to pass through, the two men slipped inside. Their footsteps echoed on the aged and in places rotting wooden floor as they made their way through the vast hall, where hundreds of world war two soldiers had lain on rows and rows of hospital cots being tended to by army nurses. The place was silent, but hummed with memories.

When they reached the door leading into the separate section at the northern end of the structure, they opened it gingerly and stepped into what appeared, from the plethora of old lighting fixtures in the centre of the room, to have been used as an operating theatre. There was another door to the left of the room, and to the far right, a set of rickety timber stairs led to a second storey. Treading carefully, the men headed toward the stairs, only to stop at the sight of a swag on the floor under the stairwell. A motorcycle helmet rested beside it, surrounded by empty beer cans.

One of the men picked up a can. It was still cool and damp. He passed it to his companion who nodded, and both pulled out their hand guns. One had a snub-nose thirty-eight special, the other a nine millimetre Glock. They made their way over to the swag and one of them nudged it with the toe of his shoe.

They were looking up the stairs when a voice rasped behind them, 'Hey.'

The man on the left spun around, gun raised, and copped a hard right hook to the nose. Stumbling backward, he fell to the floor in the corner, dazed. As his comrade whirled to face their attacker, a pair of freckled, age-creased hands grabbed his revolver and he was swung into the wall beside the stairwell.

When he tried to rise, he was pounded by a left and then a right hook to the face, followed by a powerful uppercut to his chin that sent his head slamming into the wall. When he fell to the floor unconscious, his attacker turned and advanced on the stirring man in the corner.

———

In the Globemaster, Modeen, Spooky, Wolf and Ben huddled around James at a counter fixed to the back of the cockpit wall. James was hunched over the laptop computer, squinting at the screen and tapping on the keyboard.

On Ben's orders, the agents had suited up in their HALO and night ops gear and had discarded most of the contents of their camouflage backpacks. While donning his own equipment, Ben had barked, 'Only take what we need for tonight's drop.'

Straightening and catching Ben's eye, James announced, 'I've completed my interrogation of the computer.'

Ben gave a brisk nod and raised an eyebrow. 'And?'

'Mr Williams did a good job on it, I haven't found any references to the trawler or Akeem Jibril either. It's just a standard Windows Eight laptop, no unusual hidden files and nothing out of the ordinary. It's registered to a guy named "Jabalah" whose files – luckily – were all in English.' He dug into a pocket and pulled out a small USB device which he handed to Ben. 'If you find another computer you want me to scrutinise, I don't have to be on the ground, so to speak,' and he gave a wry grin, 'to do it. Just plug this into the machine and give me a call.'

Ben nodded his thanks and put a hand on James' shoulder. 'They'll be lowering the ramp shortly, so I need you up front with the pilots. After the drop they'll be refuelling in Cairns and then heading back to Melbourne.'

'Right-o.' James began casually shutting down the laptop and gathering up his gear, but when Ben leaned closer and snapped, 'I mean NOW, James,' he found a new urgency. Throwing his gear together and bundling it haphazardly into his arms, he sprang to his feet and scurried to the cockpit, almost tripping in his haste.

Spreading a detailed map of Port Douglas on the

counter James had just vacated, Ben patted it flat with a large hand. As the others huddled around him, he pointed to a spot on the map. 'The house is right here, next to this tributary branch off Packers Creek. A satellite image taken four hours ago showed six guards and three vehicles outside. I believe the hostages are contained in a central room inside the building. Bugs should be in position on the trawler and will wave us in with a red signal on our approach.' Ben pointed to a clearing near the house. 'We'll land here, make our way through this section of bush, and take the guards out as quickly and quietly as we can. Remember, the hostages are our first priority.' He swept the others with a significant glance. 'The rebels might kill them if they're alerted to our presence, so we have to be invisible and swift.'

At the deafening sound of a buzzer, all four heads jerked upright as the glare of red flashing lights illuminated the massive cavern, making it feel more like a disco than a cargo hold. They slipped on their helmets as the fuselage decompressed and the back ramp began to lower. At Ben's nod, they turned in unison and walked toward the opening at the rear of the enormous plane. The large red lights next to the ramp flashed twice and then went a solid warning red.

Modeen pressed the comms button on her helmet and looked at Ben. 'I'm familiar with Port Douglas,' she said, her voice sounding nasal through the comms unit. At his nod, she added, 'I'll lead the jump,' and moved to the front of the group.

When the lights changed from red to unbroken green, she ran and leapt off the back of the ramp, her arms outstretched in a crucifix. At thirty thousand feet the freezing night air hit her like a brick as the Globemaster left her in its roaring wake. She hung horizontal for a spilt second while getting her bearings, then, sweeping back her arms, she rocketed earthward at a forty-five degree angle. Ben, Wolf, and Spooky followed close behind her in tight formation.

Gazing downward while spearing through the atmosphere at terminal velocity, Modeen traced the line from the mouth of the inlet to the branch off Packers Creek. Glimpsing the faint glow of a red light circling below, she banked left to zero-in on its location and checked her altitude.

Sixteen thousand.

Fifteen thousand.

Fourteen thousand.

Clenching her fist, she held up her left arm and the three men immediately broke formation behind her and spread out. As she flattened her descent, she reached behind with her right hand feeling for her drogue.

Three …

Two …

One.

She deployed her chute.

The others followed suit and four black ram-air chutes filled with air as the jumpers circled their target. Gliding silently downward, suspended from the dark wing above her, Modeen could just make out a faint rectangular shape of a house. She pulled down the night vision visor on her helmet and pressed the comms button.

'I can only make out one guard and one vehicle in the back yard.'

The others deployed their visors and Ben growled, 'Damn it, we might be too late.' He gave a frustrated sigh and muttered, 'It's more than likely they've moved the hostages,' before becoming businesslike again. 'Right, JD, you're with Bugs on the trawler. I'll take the guard in the backyard. Spook, Wolf, you're with me.'

The three men immediately banked left as Modeen went right. Taking a wide berth around the mangroves, she cut across the main arm of Packers Creek at the rear of the target property.

From the trawler's deck, Bugs continued waving the torch into the sky above, and watched as an ominous black shadow sailed silently overhead and then circled to swoop along the river toward him. The figure momentarily disappeared from view below the bow of the trawler, then rose sharply as Modeen pulled down hard on the steering toggles. The chute stalled and she landed lightly on the front deck.

Ben homed in on the guard standing at the end of

the mangrove-lined path that led to where the trawler was moored. Swooping in low down the side of the house to cover his approach, Ben turned sharply and skimmed across the lushly lawned backyard, preparing to plough his solid six foot four frame into the guard.

At the faint rush of air behind him, the man turned just as Ben lifted an elbow and caught him squarely under the chin with a bone-crushing blow, sending the guard flying. As he sailed backward, the man lost his grip on his assault rifle. He crashed to the ground with a heavy thud to lie unconscious on the lawn, his limbs askew.

On the deck of the trawler, Modeen unclipped her chute as Bugs pushed the silken nylon fabric aside with his feet. Without saying a word, she handed him a pair of night vision goggles and they made their way down the gangway and along the track toward the house. Hunched over, they emerged cautiously from the trees to see Spooky and Wolf heading to where Ben squatted beside the supine guard.

When they got closer, Modeen could see that Ben had bound the man's wrists and ankles together with thick plastic cable ties. To signal for the others to gather, she caught their attention and gave a circular twirl of her index finger and then thumped her fist into her other palm. The four men moved in close to her until the team was like a group of football players in a tight huddle.

'Their stronghold in Katoomba was wired with

explosives,' she whispered urgently. 'This place might be the same.'

Ben nodded. 'Copy that.' Straightening, he gestured for them to follow and headed toward the house.

As the team approached the dwelling, they saw only one light shining from a back room. Ben paused and held up two fingers of his right hand. He waved that arm twice pointing with his fingers, indicating the right side of the building. Wolf and Modeen peeled off from the group and skirted around to that side. When Ben waved his arm again, Spooky and Bugs peeled off to the left and disappeared into the darkness.

Modeen stopped near the first window they encountered and flattened herself against the wall. The window was half open and a central light glowed from within. Raising her night vision goggles, she took a careful scan of the empty room.

An old sleep-out by the look of it.

Moving closer, she checked the window mechanism for wires.

Clear.

With Wolf covering her from the outside, she passed her MP5 through the open window and placed it carefully on the floor inside before easing herself through the opening. As soon as she was clear, Wolf followed her in.

A central corridor ran the length of the house, with another large room at the other end. The corridor was faintly lit but the rest of the house was in darkness.

Modeen flattened herself against the wall next to the corridor, then quickly jerked her head through the entranceway to take a peek.

Clear.

She moved diagonally across the corridor and found the first door to her left open. She halted and peered into the room. It was in darkness and silent. But when she took a tentative step inside, a large pair of hands grabbed her MP5 and she was spun around and flung across the room. She landed with a thud beneath the window sill, her back against the wall. Shaking her head to clear her vision, she looked up as a large silhouette in the doorway hurled her weapon into a corner of the room. Reaching into her vest, she pulled out her Walther PPX and was palming back the slide when she caught the glint of a long, thick bowie knife.

Raising his knife hand, her assailant charged at her in the darkness just as Wolf burst into the room behind him and kept coming, pounding a heavy, well-aimed boot into the middle of the guard's back. With a house-shuddering crash, the man's solid six foot frame smashed through the window above her. She covered her head with both arms as shards of glass rained down around her.

When she looked up, she was pleased to find Wolf standing over her. He extended a hand and helped her to her feet before turning and moving to the doorway. Modeen retrieved her MP5 and they stepped into the corridor, where Spooky and Bugs joined them.

Spooky tilted his head toward the other end of the corridor. 'The rest is clear. Your guy must've been only guard left in the house.'

Wolf walked to the back door and inspected it for wires. Satisfied it wasn't booby-trapped, he unlocked it and pulled it open. Sticking out his head, he looked left and then right, as Ben appeared around the corner of the house, dragging Modeen's assailant by the collar of his bloodied shirt. Once inside, Ben lifted off his night vision goggles and dropped the man beneath the light.

The guard writhed in a slick of his own blood, gurgling and clutching his throat. Through his trembling fingers they saw a shard of window glass protruding from a gushing three inch gash in his neck. The guy's body arched as he choked violently, coughing up thick clots of blood. At his final, frenzied spasm, his eyes went dim and his body rigid, before he sagged motionless to the bloody floor.

'Well, so much for questioning *him*,' Spooky murmured drily.

CHAPTER TWELVE

Ben turned off the light, pulled down his night vision goggles and tapped Wolf on the shoulder. 'Grab the other guard and bring him inside.'

'I'll give you a hand.' Spooky followed Wolf out the back door as Ben turned to Bugs.

'What about the guard on the boat?'

'He's not gonna be any good to us either.' Bugs gave an apologetic shrug. 'I thought there'd be others left we could interrogate.'

With a disgruntled snort, Ben turned to stride through the house, his night vision goggles casting a vivid green tinge to his surroundings. Bugs and Modeen followed close behind, their weapons still at the ready.

Ben paused in the centre of the corridor and shook his head. 'This doesn't make any sense. There should be a central room where the hostages were being held.

The three men showed up on the thermal satellite image as clear as day. They were right here.'

Modeen raised her eyes to the ceiling. 'The roof's too flat for there to be a loft.' She glanced at Ben and Bugs, who sprang into action as if a light bulb had turned on inside their heads.

Muttering, 'There's gotta be a trapdoor to a cellar...,' Ben disappeared into one of the side rooms. Bugs entered the opposite room while Modeen headed along the corridor to the front lounge. A large Persian floor rug caught her eye. Lifting it, she gazed at the wooden boards beneath and called, 'Bingo!'

Folding back the rug, she straightened, staring at the trapdoor, as Ben and Bugs came to stand beside her. When Bugs squatted and reached for the trapdoor handle, the hairs on back of her neck stood on end and she yelled, 'STOP!'

Bugs immediately froze as Spooky strode up behind him, saying, 'It's that damned radar of hers.'

Ben raised a hand to change his NatSec goggles from night vision to thermal imaging, and scanned the area. The heat signatures from Modeen, Wolf, Bugs, and Spooky glowed bright red and orange around their heads and body cores. Down the corridor he could see the unconscious guard Wolf had dragged in and dumped next to his dead comrade, whose cooling corpse barely gave off a dull maroon glow.

'No other heat signatures,' Ben announced, flicking his goggles back to night vision.

Modeen walked to the centre of the corridor, testing the floor with her boots. 'This floorboard's a bit loose.'

Handing Bugs the M4 carbine he'd taken from the guard, Wolf made his way to Modeen's side. Pulling his bayonet from its scabbard, he knelt and thrust the blade between the crack of the loose floorboard, prying it upward. It gave a little, so he kept the pressure on as Ben knelt and worked his bayonet into the other side of the floorboard. When the board lifted, Spooky grabbed it by the end. Using the power in his legs he straightened, bending the hoop-pine board backward and snapping it in half.

Ben rose and used the heel of his boot to stomp two more floorboards, shattering them. Wolf did the same on the other side, and then knelt and reefed the broken sections free. When they'd finished, they squatted to look through the decent-sized hole they'd made in the floor. There was indeed a cellar below. Spooky dropped his body across the opening and grabbed hold of an exposed floor joist. Kicking his legs forward, he swung down and disappeared into the dark room below.

His voice rose through the hole. 'They're not here.' His last few words were muffled. Moments later, he emerged through the trap door in the lounge room holding a cube of C4 explosive. Pulling out the detonator, he threw the cube to Modeen. 'But I did find this.'

Ben clapped her on the shoulder. 'Good call, JD.'

'Yeah, thanks Modeen.' Bugs gave her the thumbs-up signal.

She acknowledged their gratitude with a nod. 'So what do we do now? We've got no idea where they've taken the hostages.'

Bugs gave a toothy grin. 'Don't we?'

They all turned to stare at him and Ben barked, 'Well?'

Still grinning, he replied, 'You guys don't call me Bugs for nothin' ya know. All we need is a NatSec laptop and we can track 'em.'

'What's the tracking number?' Ben pulled out his mobile as Modeen, Wolf and Spooky did the same.

Bugs frowned quizzically at them. 'TD5032, 5033 and 5034, but you can't track 'em using your pho—' He bit back the last words as Ben held his smart phone in front of Bugs' face.

On the dial, three tiny blue dots beeped on a Google map image. Lowering his mobile, Ben zoomed in on the dots and studied them, muttering to Bugs as he did so, 'We need to upgrade your phone.' He reached up a hand to slap him on the back. 'But good work, mate.'

'Looks like one of their vehicles is in Atherton, and the other is just outside of Tolga.' Modeen glanced at Ben. 'Now all we need is transport.'

'TD5032 is still parked outside,' Bugs said, 'and my hire car is in town near the boat ramp.'

Spooky leaned forward and whispered, 'Car.'

'Yes, a car. I hired one.' Bugs frowned, thinking Spooky wasn't usually so dense.

'No!' Spooky said in a harsh whisper as he raced to

the front window. 'I hear a car. It's coming up the driveway.'

At those words, Wolf yanked the slide back on his M4 and released it as he and Bugs moved swiftly into position next to the front window opposite Spooky. Modeen flattened herself against the wall beside the side window as Ben hastened down the corridor. For a big man, he leaped with surprising lightness over the hole in the floor, before disappearing out the back door.

'White four wheel drive,' Spooky whispered, 'just pulled up. The guy's sitting inside, appears to be waiting.'

Wolf lifted the window a crack and stuck the carbine's muzzle through it, only to have Bugs put a restraining hand on his arm.

'Ease up, big fella. The guy's on our side. That's Salty in my hire car.'

Wolf withdrew his weapon and the others relaxed as Bugs went to the front door and let himself out. As he walked toward the car, Salty got out and met him halfway, saying cheerfully, 'Good to see you're still alive and kickin' young fella. Thought you might need your vehicle.'

Bugs clapped him on the back. 'Onya Salty.'

'When I snuck along the drive and saw all was quiet, I figured it was OK to come right up to the house.'

'Salty! Good to see you, old mate.' Ben materialised from the shadowy darkness.

'Ben, you too.' The two men shook hands and Salty asked, 'Is there anything I can do?'

'You've already done a lot, but yes, you can help with one more thing. We've got two terrorists down and one tied up in the house. We need to make tracks, so can you alert the Feds about them after we've gone? Can't afford to waste time hanging around here answering questions.'

'No problem Ben, consider it done. Now, I could use a ride to the boat ramp?' Salty began making his way back toward the car, the pearl pistol grip of a gold Desert Eagle just visible above the waistband of his pants.

Ben turned to Bugs. 'Drop Salty at the ramp. We'll see if we can find the keys to their other vehicle.' He jerked a thumb toward the Black 4WD parked next to the house.

When Bugs arrived back at the house after letting Salty off at the boat ramp, the black 4WD was in the driveway with its lights on. At his approach, Spooky and Modeen got out of the vehicle and walked toward him. He stopped beside them and Modeen reached for the door handle.

'How about I drive for a bit? I know where we're going, and you look like you could use some sleep.'

'Yeah, right-o.' Bugs got out and went around to the passenger side.

Seating himself in the back, Spooky leaned between the front seats to tell Bugs, 'Looks like the Bedford van is parked just outside Tolga at Rocky Creek. But it's got me why the hell they've gone there.'

'It's actually a bit insulting,' Modeen mumbled.

'Insulting? How?'

'Well, from memory Rocky Creek is the site of an old world war two military hospital, Australia's largest in fact. The terrorists' presence there is an insult to all diggers.'

Bugs gave a snort. 'You're a font of knowledge, Modeen, I'm impressed.'

'Don't be. I just happened to camp in the caravan park near the site on my way up to Cooktown once, and of course I had to check out the old abandoned Nissan hut.' Modeen looked thoughtful. 'That's pretty much all that's left of the hospital now.' She sat straighter. 'Anyway, we need to get moving. Ben reckons we must have the terrorists rattled, otherwise they'd be spruiking and making all sorts of demands.'

Putting the car into gear, she said, 'We'll head out of Port Douglas toward Mossman, then go up the Rex Range. It's the quickest route.'

The hostages sat on the filthy floor, backs against the wall, hands resting in their laps with their wrists firmly strapped together. The air in the dingy room was thick with dust and the stench of decay and rodent. In one corner, rusting army cots stacked against the wall were festooned with spider webs. A mattress had been thrown on top of the stack, its blue and white striped ticking faded and dotted with holes. Out of one of these, a rat poked its head and then hastily retreated.

Azeez and Aldin stood over the hostages. Both men sported impressive bruising on their faces, and Azeez had a trail of dried blood below his swollen and now crooked nose. He sniffed, ran a hand over his injured face, and winced.

Swallowing a grin at the thought their captors had been given some of their own medicine, Sir Robert mustered his courage, sat straighter and said with a show of bravado, 'I say, where have you taken our friend?'

'Shut up, *dog!*' Azeez stepped forward and struck him on the side of the head with the butt of his rifle.

Sir Robert gave a grunt of pain and slumped against Mike Johnston. As he regained his composure, he whispered, 'Where do you think they've taken Modeen?'

Mike remained silent and threw the guard an anxious glance, not wanting to antagonise the irate man further.

'I said QUIET!' This time Azeez stepped in and kicked Sir Robert in the thigh with the toe of his boot.

'Alright, alright.' Sir Robert flinched and rubbed his leg, as the sound of a vehicle arriving outside reached their ears.

Doors opened and closed, and heavy footsteps could be heard crossing the wooden ramp at the front of the building.

Azeez turned to Aldin and flicked his head toward the noise. 'The reinforcements have arrived.'

With a curt nod, Aldin left the room, his footsteps echoing hollowly as he strode the length of the empty hall. Inside the main doors, he stopped in front of four solidly-built young men. They were all olive-skinned with heavily jelled black hair, and wore dark tee-shirts over low-slung pants. Their under-pants were visible, protruding from the waistbands of their jeans. All four sported insolent expressions and two had lit cigarettes dangling from their fingers.

Aldin eyed them sceptically, thinking two of them looked physically fit at least. 'Have these men had any training?' he asked a shadowy figure standing behind them.

Not waiting for the boss to answer, the tallest of the four stepped forward and bowed to Aldin. 'We are eager to serve and devoted to the Spear of Allah.'

From behind them the shadowy figure commanded, 'I want three men standing sentry outside all night.' He spoke with a broad Australian twang. 'At dawn I want everyone inside. Keep quiet and don't draw any attention to the place.'

Aldin frowned. 'Where are you going?'

'To make arrangements for another location.'

'But why are you taking the third one?'

'He's not part of this deal, but may prove useful.' The boss stepped forward and his dark eyes glinted in the shadows. 'Remember, we need the hostages alive for the exchange. I'll call when I've secured a safer place.' He dropped a duffel bag at Aldin's feet and it hit the floor with a heavy metallic thump. 'Here, distribute these.'

Aldin bowed his head. 'As you command.' Kneeling, he opened the duffel, handed AK47 assault rifles to three of the new recruits and took one for himself. To the fourth, tallest recruit, he passed the remaining nine millimetre Browning pistol.

Bugs woke from his power nap as Modeen bounced the 4WD along the rocky track. He stretched his tall frame, yawned, and looked out the window into the darkness of early morning. The sky above them was clear, speckled with a mass of stars. 'Where are we?'

'About seven hundred metres north of the Nissan hut,' Modeen replied. 'It's just across that gully.' She nosed the vehicle onto a flat, level clearing.

'Where did you get this?' Spooky said from the back seat.

Bugs glanced over his shoulder to see Spooky holding a Barrett sniper rifle on his lap and looking well pleased as he stroked the rifle's barrel.

'I might've been out of the country for a while,' Bugs grinned, 'but I've still got my contacts.'

Grinning, Spooky turned to Modeen. "What did I tell you? The boy's got skills.'

Ben pulled up beside them in the black 4WD they had seized from the Port Douglas homestead. As he and Wolf got out, he gestured for them all to assemble behind the vehicle. Opening the rear door of the 4WD, he grabbed his backpack and pulled out five tiny comms units. After handing them out, he fitted the remaining unit snuggly into his own ear.

Spooky held up the Barrett to show Wolf. 'Look what we've got.'

Wolf's eyes strained to see in the gloom. 'Is that an

82A1?' When Spooky handed him the rifle, Wolf put it close to the 4WD's tail lights to get a clearer view. He extracted the magazine from the base of the weapon and weighed it in his hand, then pulled back the slide and checked the action, crooning, 'Sweeet.'

'Right, gather round.' Ben pulled out his phone and brought up a Google Earth map. Placing a thumb and finger on the screen, he spread them apart to zoom in on the structure in the centre of the map. 'We're here and the hostages are presumed to be in this Nissan hut. But I'm not familiar with the area or the terrain.' He threw Modeen a questioning glance.

She raised an eyebrow at Wolf. 'Firstly you can leave that canon behind. The ground surrounding the hut is flat and thick with trees and low shrubs. No high vantage points or clearings for a long shot.'

Wolf frowned and his shoulders slumped.

Spooky slapped him on his broad back. 'Next time, buddy.'

'Spook, you're point,' Ben barked, 'and Wolf, I want you to circle round and cover the south. JD, you're east and Bugs, west. I'll cover the north.'

They checked their weapons and Modeen pressed a finger to her comms unit. 'Comms check, Modeen.'

The others followed suit, sounding off.

'Comms check, Ben.'

'Check, Wolf.'

'Comms check, Bugs.'

'Check Spooky.'

'Remember, stealth at all times.' Ben's deep, commanding voice crackled through the comms units. 'If we're "made", we need to get to the hostages ASAP. We can't afford to give the insurgents cause or opportunity to harm them.'

'Just like old times,' Spooky muttered as he pulled down his night vision goggles and disappeared into the gully, followed close behind by Wolf.

Ben turned to the others. 'We'll give them two minutes' start.'

They waited in pent-up silence until Ben moved forward, raising a hand and indicating for them to follow. They headed down the gully, keeping low with Ben in the lead, Modeen on his left and Bugs on his right. As they neared the site, the silhouette of the Nissan hut came into view.

Even in the dark, it was an unusual shape. In contrast to the elongated, semi-circular-roofed main hall, a double storey rectangular structure appeared tacked on to the building's northern end. When they got closer, they could see shuttered windows along the full length of the hall, providing ventilation for the dark, cavernous interior. The shutters were twisted and crumbling with age, and the winding mechanisms had corroded long ago, locking the windows into the fully open position. The corrugated iron panels covering the roof and external walls wore a patina of deep red rust, and one section of roofing had collapsed inward.

'Three guards outside,' Spooky whispered over the

comms. 'One north, one south and the other on the eastern side. The van's parked in the north-east corner and there's a motorbike in the bushes on the western side. No sign of the other 4WD.'

Ben grunted his understanding. 'It's a good bet the hostages are still here. Can you make out numbers inside the hut?'

'Two armed guards in the hall,' Spooky whispered. 'Not sure about the double storey section at the northern end.' His next words were punctuated with a whoosh of air. 'Give me a minute.' He crept down the western side of the building and disappeared between thick shrubs.

The main part of the hut had been built a metre off the ground and rested on solid concrete stumps, a legacy of an upgrade some years before. Spotting a gap in the thick, unkempt shrubs that surrounded the building and made for excellent cover, Spooky crawled on all fours underneath the northern end of the building. Once in position, he rolled onto his back and put his hand to his night vision goggles, intending to switch the view to thermal imaging. When his fingers didn't find the switch, he rolled his eyes and swore under his breath.

Freakin' Robson, cheapskate. Y'coulda given us the combo goggles.

Shoving the goggles on top of his head, he pulled out his phone. Tapping on the thermal imaging app, he used the phone to scan upward from beneath the floorboards. After studying the images it revealed, he clicked off the app. Knowing if he spoke he might be heard by the guards, he sent Ben a text.

2 hostages

1 guard north block

Outside, Ben's phone vibrated with an incoming message. He signalled to Modeen and Bugs and they peeled off to the east and west of the building as he pulled his phone out and dropped back down the gully.

He read the message and then pressed a finger to his earpiece. 'Can you get a clear shot at the guard in with the hostages, Spook?' Seconds later his phone buzzed again with another incoming message.

Yes

'Right team,' Ben barked into his comms unit, 'on my mark we'll neutralise the sentries then take up positions on the east and west side of the hall. There are two guards inside, try to wing them. When the shooting starts, Spook, I want you to take out the guard in the room with the hostages.' Taking a deep breath, he commanded, 'Go.'

Spooky flicked off the safety on his M4 carbine and with his right hand, pointed its muzzle toward the floorboards above his head. In his left hand, he raised his phone and focused the thermal imaging app on the guard. The man was standing near the door, in between Spooky and the hostages.

On the eastern side of the building, Modeen crept

forward to take cover behind a large tree, twenty metres from the side wall of the Nissan hut. The nearest guard was five metres in front of her, shuffling his feet and stretching his arms across his body as if warming up for a marathon. Squatting, she picked up a rock and threw it into the bushes a few metres behind and to the side of her position.

When the guard heard the rock hit the shrubbery and then roll over dry leaf matter on the ground, he moved to investigate. As soon as he drew level with the tree, Modeen leaped out and struck him with a Karate chop to the throat. When the man gasped, choked and bent double clutching his throat, she followed through with a kick to his head, knocking him to the ground. Once certain he was out cold, she rolled him over and bound his wrists and ankles with cable ties she took from her boot.

Sitting on her haunches, she placed a finger on her earpiece and whispered, 'East guard down.'

On the southern side of the building, Wolf crept up behind the guard who was pacing up and down, smoking and muttering to himself as he marched. When the man went to turn and head back the other way, Wolf knocked him out with a right cross to his chin.

Moments later, the others heard his gravelly whisper over the comms. 'Southern guard down.'

Ben crept up behind the sentry on the northern side. The young man was standing by a tree, facing south, urinating. He leaned on the trunk with one hand, and had propped his AK47 against his leg. There was low but dense shrubbery between them. Ben knew he couldn't creep up on the guy, he'd have to take him on the run. His muscles bunched and he hurdled the shrubs. Flying toward the man, he hit him full force with an elbow to the back of the head.

The guard fell headfirst into the tree, then ricocheted backward and slumped to the ground unconscious.

'Northern guard down,' Ben muttered into his comms unit.

CHAPTER FOURTEEN

Bugs peered inside. He was stationed outside the western side of the building roughly halfway down the length of the huge hall. Through the rotting wooden shutters and their panels of chicken wire, he could see the guard positioned inside, in the far corner. The man was leaning back against the wall, an AK47 in his hands and a nine millimetre Glock shoved down the front of his pants.

Modeen took up position outside a window on the eastern side, opposite Bugs. From there, she could see the guard stationed inside the hall, in the opposite corner. He had jelled black hair and was gazing down at a Browning pistol in his hands as though fascinated with the weapon.

Watching him she mused, *this guy's definitely not army.*

Wolf stood five metres back from the double doors

at the building's southern entrance. He pressed his comms unit. 'Wolf. In position.'

Ben whispered, 'Ready.'

The guard with the Browning finished his inspection of the weapon. Holding it in his right hand, he crossed his arms and raised his chin, looking poised to take on the world.

Seeing him, Aldin barked, 'Point that thing the other way, *idiot!*'

Throwing him an apologetic glance, the man shifted the weapon to his left hand and once more folded his arms across his chest. He had just settled back against the wall when Modeen let loose a three-round burst from her MP5, shattering his left hand. The Browning clattered to the floor as the guard reeled, staring at the ragged, meaty stump at the end of his left arm, and wailed in agony.

Aldin had snapped to attention at the gunshot but was hit hard in the left shoulder and thrown against the wall when Bugs fired a round from his M4. Sliding down the wall, leaving a wet crimson smear on it, Aldin dropped his AK47 to the floor. At that moment, the front doors to the hall burst open and off their hinges and the big, dark shape of Wolf stood silhouetted in the opening.

In the hostages' room, Azeez whirled toward the captives, his weapon raised. Beneath the floorboards, Spooky fired three short burst of his assault rifle, ripping shards and splinters of wood off the floorboards as he strafed a stunned Azeez in the chest. The two hostages cowered, covering their heads with their arms, as Azeez slumped to the floor in a bloody heap.

Standing menacingly in the entrance to the hall with his M4 in his hand, Wolf bellowed, 'Don't move!'

Ignoring him, Aldin fumbled for his Glock. Seeing that, Bugs let loose another round and Aldin slumped to the floor, the back of his head gone.

Ben raced up the northern stairs and crashed through the side door. It crumpled under the force of his charge as though made of cardboard. He marched across the old theatre room, checking left to right. Entering the room holding the hostages, he pulled out his Glock and knelt over Azeez checking for a pulse. Satisfied, he rose and moved toward the hostages.

'You're safe now gentleman.' He knelt and cut their bonds.

'Oh,' Sir Robert sighed, 'thank heavens. And thank you.'

Ben took off his night vision goggles and turned on the battery-powered lantern Azeez had set up in the room earlier.

In the hall, Wolf wrapped a tourniquet around the sobbing guard's bleeding arm, then sat him on the floor and strapped his ankles together with a thick cable tie. Glancing at the man's tear-streaked face, he growled, 'Shouldn't play with guns.' He picked up the Browning and walked over to check on Aldin.

Bugs, Spooky and Modeen strode across the hall

and through the door into the old theatre room at the northern end of the building. Modeen and Bugs went left and joined Ben in the room with the hostages while Spooky turned right and sprinted up the stairs to check the top level.

Modeen swept a glance around the room and then looked at Sir Robert. 'Where's d—' she bit back the word. 'The other hostage?'

Sir Robert rolled his eyes and took a deep breath. 'As I was just telling your friend here, John was in the van with us when we arrived at this place. Then Michael and I were thrown into this room. We don't know what they did with poor John.' He frowned. 'I do hope he's alright.'

Modeen left the room and met Spooky at the bottom of the stairs. 'Anything up there?' she asked hopefully.

'Nothing.' Spooky shook his head at her but was looking down at the floor. 'What do ya suppose happened with this old digger?' With a tilt of his chin he indicated a grey-haired man sprawled on his side under the stairs beside a blood-splattered swag.

Modeen moved closer and squatted beside the man. He lay pale and still, with dark blotches of blood on his khaki tee-shirt and camouflage cargo pants. From the top pocket of his sleeveless denim jacket a Triumph motorcycle emblem dangled on a chain, and beside the swag she saw a motorcycle helmet and a khaki flak jacket sporting numerous military medals. On the shoulder of the jacket was a green insignia with a central blue stripe, and on his arm a tattoo read *ADF 3rdBrig 1stBatt.*

'He's an old Vietnam vet, Third Brigade, First Battalion. Light Infantryman, from Lavarack Barracks.' She hung her head. 'What a shame. Looks like he put up a good fight.' She lifted one of his freckled hands. 'Check out the blood under his nails and broken skin on his knuckles.'

Spooky nodded. 'Yeah. He did well right up to the point where he got a bullet in the head. Guess there's worse ways for an old soldier to go.'

They heard Ben barking orders into his mobile. 'Chopper at this location, ASAP.' There was a pause and then he growled, 'Well then wake him! This is a matter of national security. Call me back in five minutes, and you'd better have some good news.'

Spooky joined Ben and the others in the hostages' room, where Wolf was busy checking the two captives while Ben paced the floor, talking on the phone.

Snapping shut his mobile's case, Ben turned to the others. 'Just waiting on transport, they should be able to get an army chopper here within the hour from Townsville HQ—'

He was interrupted by the sound of a large motor-cycle starting up outside. It revved and accelerated, flicking up gravel before snaking along the narrow dirt track. They heard it hit the asphalt and then speed northward for a short burst.

Ben frowned at the others. 'JD?'

Spooky slipped out to check the old diggers' pockets and returned to nod at Ben. 'Yep, she's taken old mate's keys and his helmet.'

At that moment Bugs entered the room, dragging behind him one of the sentries from outside. 'You chasin' JD?' He inclined his head toward the outside. 'Just saw her headin' to where we left the vehicles.'

Ben put a finger to his earpiece. 'JD.'

No reply.

'JD.'

Silence greeted him again.

'JD, respond.'

He walked to the southern entrance of the Nissan hut just in time to see the lights of the Triumph as it rocketed past on the main highway heading south. The dark figure of its rider was sitting low across the tank and neatly tucked behind the faring as the big bike continued gathering speed. Taking out his phone, Ben brought up the Google Earth map. The blue blip that was the terrorists' 4WD vehicle was heading east toward Yungaburra and the Gillies Highway.

'Dammit, she's going after him.' He threw Spooky a set of keys. 'You and Bugs better back her up.'

Spooky caught the keys on the run. He shot out of the room, sprinted across the gully and returned shortly afterward driving the black 4WD Ben and Wolf had arrived in earlier. Buzzing down the window as

Bugs jumped into the passenger side, he shouted to Ben, 'She's taken the Barrett.'

'Great,' Ben muttered drily with a shake of his head. He glanced at his watch. 'It'll be dawn in a couple of hours. Chopper will be here in forty-five. Keep me posted on your progress.'

Spinning the 4WD around, Spooky slammed his foot on the accelerator and the vehicle fishtailed along the gravel road toward the highway.

CHAPTER FIFTEEN

Tucked behind the bikini faring of the old digger's 1200cc Triumph Tiger, Modeen lay against the tank out of the wind. She had her NatSec phone wedged between the speedo and the faring, and the Barrett sniper rifle slung over her shoulder so it rested snugly against her back. At that time of night, she had the road to herself. Flicking her eyes down to the phone every now and then, she monitored the blue dot's progress on the Google Earth map. It was heading along the Gillies Highway toward Yungaburra.

I'll take Marks Lane, it'll be quicker.

She opened up the throttle and roared into Tolga.

'What the—' Senior constable Jim MacGregor jerked upright and blinked at the reading on his radar. Stunned, he took a double take.

A hundred and eighty-five kilometres per hour? You're kidding!

The bike flew past with a high-pitched wine, a rush of wind in its wake. With his eyes glued to the rapidly disappearing blur of the bike's tail lights through his vehicle's bug-spattered windscreen, MacGregor started the patrol car and reached for the light switch preparing to begin his pursuit. In his haste, he managed to break the knob off the switch as he wrenched it on. The blue and red lights on the roof of his pursuit vehicle came alive, illuminating his hiding place beside the road and engulfing the surrounding trees with an eerie pulsing glow. Throwing the radar detector onto the empty passenger's seat beside him, he whipped the car out of hiding and onto the highway, and stomped on the accelerator.

Modeen dropped the bike down two gears and slowed to a hundred and twenty as she snaked though the sleeping town of Tolga. She was still alone on the road, so was momentarily puzzled when she noticed her surroundings develop a pulsing blue tinge. Realising what it must be, she glanced at the rear view mirror and cursed, 'Shit! Not now.'

Dropping the bike down another two gears, she leaned it into a tight left hand corner, and then accelerated hard past the light industrial area, leaving the blue lights in her wake. The Triumph sailed over the railway line with barely a bump as she opened up the throttle on the long straight stretch. The bike handled well and she silently thanked the old digger for taking good care of it. But it was no road racer, she had to reduce speed considerably for tight corners, and ahead of her the straight section of road was fast coming to an end.

She bent lower over the tank and sailed into the tight bends in the road, taking them as fast as the Triumph could handle, but the blue lights appeared in her rear view mirror again. Snaking through an S bend, she raced down a dip, leaned into the curve of a narrow bridge and then powered up the incline, soaring the bike over the crest. But after another couple of tight turns, she could tell the car behind was closing the gap.

She scowled.

I haven't got time for this.

She slowed for the next corner, bringing the blue lights closer still. At the next tight bend she decreased speed further, and again for a sharp left turn and then a right into Marks Lane. By this time the pursuit car was nipping at her heels.

'Gotcha now,' MacGregor snarled under his breath as he turned on the siren.

Gritting her teeth, she accelerated hard and cut across to the opposite lane, but then jammed on the brakes. The big bike went nose-down in response, bringing the police car parallel with her.

Reaching her left hand into her vest, she pulled out Walt.

MacGregor's eyes widened in horror at the sight of the weapon, and again when he saw the pistol flash twice as she shot out his front and rear tyres, making the car judder and twitch. For good measure, she also put a bullet through the car's radiator. Hastily slowing the incapacitated vehicle, MacGregor could only watch as Modeen powered away. He swore loudly and pounded the steering wheel with both hands as his pursuit car limped to a ungainly stop on the side of the road. Even as he fumbled for the two-way, Modeen had already disappeared from view.

On the next straight stretch of road, she checked the Google Earth map on her phone. The blue blip that was the 4WD had passed through Yungaburra and was heading toward the notoriously winding Gillies Range crossing. She wrenched the throttle open and punched through the gears. The Triumph responded well, but didn't feel as stable at speed as her GTR.

She had to slow the bike through Yungaburra village, and took a moment to glance down at her phone again. The blue dot had entered the first turns on the Gillies range, but she was closing fast. After a couple of sweeping bends, she powered through the gears again, bending low over the tank and tucking her arms close to her sides and her knees firm against the Triumph's warm, thumping body.

Squeezing out every bit of power the big bike

could give her on the straights, she pushed the three cylinder machine up to two hundred and twenty kilometres an hour. The faring gave her some protection, but she could feel the wind whipping against her as the bike flew over the smooth, recently repaired bitumen.

When the first tight bend on the range came into view, she eased back the throttle and checked her phone. The 4WD was two kilometres ahead, taking it easy on the winding road, clearly oblivious it was being pursued. Leaning hard into the corners, cutting them when she dared and taking a wide line through the tight bends, she nudged closer with each turn.

She was within a kilometre of her target.

Well behind her, a black 4WD raced into Tolga.

Gazing at Spooky's smart phone, Bugs muttered, 'According to this we should take Marks Lane.'

Gripping the steering wheel firmly, Spooky flicked him a sideways glance. 'Just tell me when to turn.'

'Right-o, keep your shirt on. Ya gotta chuck a left after we pass through town.' Bugs threw him a toothy grin. 'Never a dull moment with you guys.' And a short time later, 'Left here. Now!'

Spooky slammed on the brakes and changed down through the gears as he threw the big 4WD into a tight left turn. Bugs braced himself against the door and his seat as they careered around the corner, all-terrain tyres howling on the bitumen.

With a bark of laughter he yelled, 'Now sting the big tupster! Let's see what she can do.' Leaning toward Spooky, he shouted over the roar of the vehicle's powerful V8 diesel engine, 'We've got a nice long straight before we hit the chicanes.'

Flying along the straights and powering through the bends, they made good time. As they took a right turn onto Marks Lane, they saw a white police car parked on the roadside ahead.

Flicking Bugs a frown, Spooky snarled through his teeth, 'This we *don't* need.'

When they drew closer and saw how low the pursuit vehicle was sitting on two nearside flat tyres, and the steam billowing from its shattered grille, they both grinned. There was no way that car was going to give chase. But their relief was short-lived when their headlights illuminated a policeman standing in the middle of the road. He had one arm raised in a halting gesture while his other hand rested on his side arm.

Bugs turned to Spooky. 'What do we do now?'

Throwing the car down a gear, Spooky stomped hard on the accelerator, muttering, 'He won't shoot.' When MacGregor dived out of the way of the charging vehicle, Spooky snorted. 'Told ya. There's too much paper work involved.'

Bugs frowned. 'Two blown tyres *and* a blown radiator. Coincidence?'

'Nah.' Spooky chuckled. 'The Modeen factor, I reckon. That copper's just lucky she didn't have time to stop.' Winding up the big 4WD down the straight, taking it to redline in every gear, he said to Bugs, 'You wanna give Ben an update?'

'OK, but there's not much to report so far.' Bugs pressed a couple of icons on the phone and scrolled through the contact list.

CHAPTER SIXTEEN

Modeen could see flashes of the 4WD's tail lights ahead as it snaked its way down the winding range. The narrow two-laned road hugged the jagged edges of the escarpment and in places dropped away alarmingly mere inches past the edge of the bitumen. Not the best place to tackle another vehicle, she decided, especially one likely to be carrying precious cargo. And the driver wouldn't be inclined to meekly pull over at her request, of that she was convinced.

A glint of headlights through the trees to her right caught her eye and she raised her head to look over the deep crevasse. She saw an oncoming vehicle appear around a tight bend. It was probably three kilometres away by road, but across the chasm was only about nine hundred metres from her current position. At that point on the range crossing, the mountainous terrain meant the sections of road snaked close to each other.

In that instant, she formed a plan of attack.

Braking hard, she pulled the bike off the road onto a narrow strip above the escarpment, the skidding tyres sending a shower of gravel over the edge. Steadying the Triumph with her feet, she flicked off the headlights, killed the motor, and dropped her helmet to the ground. Moving swiftly, she dipped her shoulder and slung the Barrett from her back, pulling back and releasing the slide in one fluid movement.

The first one hundred and thirty-eight millimetre long bullet slipped smoothly into the chamber. Sliding back on the bike's seat, she rested the rifle barrel on top of the faring.

The steep hillside sloping upward from the road across the chasm provided a perfect backdrop for a test shot. The oncoming vehicle was climbing the short stretch of straight road in her field of vision. Leaning forward, she aimed the cross hairs of the scope on a small rock at the base of the hillside and let loose the first round.

Peering through the rifle's large scope, she counted.

One, and—

A puff of pale dust exploded next to the rock as the bullet found its mark.

Two inches high and half an inch to the right.

She did the calculations in her head, but then saw the black 4WD pass the oncoming vehicle at the top of the straight.

No time to adjust the scope.

Taking a deep breath, she put the cross hairs in front of the 4WD's nearside wheel.

If I can shoot out a front tyre, the driver will be forced to pull over. Then I might be able to take him out without fear of harming Dad.

She breathed out and focused her whole being on making the shot. The 4WD was halfway down the straight when she let loose the second round.

One, and—

She watched through the scope as the base of the front tyre blew and the 4WD zigzagged sharply left and then right.

He'll have to pull up now.

But as she watched, aghast, the big vehicle appeared to accelerate.

Oh no, no….

She sucked in a breath as the 4WD missed the sharp U turn at the jutting crest of the winding road, went sideways in the gravel, and then straightened and disappeared off the edge of the escarpment into the trees and rocks below.

Screaming, 'DAD!' she slung the rifle onto her back again, started the big bike and spun it out of the gravel and onto the road, the back tyre snaking as it searched for grip under the vigorous acceleration.

She sped past the oncoming car. It was only a watery blur to her fearful eyes. Cutting the corners, she raced down the incline to where the 4WD had left the road. Slamming on the brakes, she threw the bike sideways and jumped off, letting the Triumph drop on its side, wheels still spinning.

Pulling her night vision goggles up from around her neck, she slipped them over her eyes and ran to the edge of the cliff to scan the terrain below. The first thing she saw was a glow shining downward. The 4WD had come to rest twenty metres down the escarpment, wedged among rocks with its front grille bent around a large iron bark tree. One of its headlights was still illuminated, the other smashed. Steam hissed and gurgled from the vehicle's radiator and crumpled bonnet, and a raised back wheel spun morosely in the air. She looked closer. The front door of the vehicle was open and she couldn't see the driver.

Yanking the Walther PPX from under her vest, she stepped off the edge and began making her way down the slope, skipping from rock to rock when she could or skidding in the scree and using the trees and shrubs to break her rapid decent.

When she was ten metres behind and to the right of the 4WD wagon, she paused, reluctant to give away her position in the darkness. Shifting her goggles to the top of her head, she pulled out her phone and pressed the 'on' button. The screen illuminated and she hastily shielded it with a hand.

May as well paint a target on my forehead, she thought crossly, *this thing stands out like a beacon in the darkness.*

She tapped on the heat imaging app and held up the phone, sweeping it in a wide scan. The heat from the vehicle's engine glowed white on the screen, and in the wrecked wagon's back compartment she could make out the faint heat signature of one person. Holding her breath, she scanned the surrounding bush to the right and front of the vehicle, and then behind her.

Nothing.

She lowered the phone, recalling its thermal imaging range of fifteen to twenty metres.

At least nothing in the immediate area.

Switching off the phone, she dragged her night vision goggles onto her face again. Pulling back and releasing the slide on the PPX, she crept toward the back of the wagon, trying for rocky footholds to avoid spraying the vehicle with gravel and alerting whoever was inside of her approach.

When she reached the wreck, she paused and grasped the rear door handle with a tentative hand. The vehicle was nose-down, at a forty-five degree angle, so the door was heavy to lift. Using both hands and all her weight, she managed to wrench it open, and then gravity caught it and rested it on its hinges.

With Walt at the ready and leading the way, she stuck her head around the door and peered inside, fearful of what she would find waiting there. The sight that met her overwhelmed her with excitement and relief. It was her father, looking wide-eyed back at her with a broad tape across his mouth and his arms and wrists bound.

Her father, alive and OK.

Reaching for him with both arms, she pulled him toward her, hugging him tightly to her chest as he made muffled sounds through the tape. She kissed him on the forehead and then pulled back. Pressing the safety on, she shoved Walt back into her vest and pulled the bayonet from the scabbard strapped to her calf. She used the blade to cut her father's bonds and then stared into his eyes. He looked dazed, confused, and in shock from his ordeal.

Lifting her night vision goggles onto the top of her head, she said gently, 'Dad it's me, Josephine. You're safe now.'

Reaching up a shaking hand, he ripped the tape from his mouth, winced, and then gazed at her in wonder. 'Josephine?' he croaked. 'Where did … how did you …?' Tears rolled down his cheeks as she pulled him close again and hugged him tight.

Their brief moment of joy was broken by the sound of an approaching vehicle squealing to a halt on the road above them. They both froze. Then, with a significant glance at her father and putting a finger to her lips, she pulled Walt from her vest. They remained still and silent as doors opened and closed above and they heard two men speaking urgently. Recognising the voices, Modeen exhaled with relief and put Walt away.

'It's OK Dad, they're with me.'

Moments later Spooky and Bugs had clambered down the hillside and stood outside the wreck.

Reefing open the other rear door, Bugs said, 'You OK, Modeen?' When she and her father both answered, 'Yes,' he chuckled, adding, 'Good. Ben's organised a chopper, ETA about 20 minutes.'

Modeen held her father at arm's length, running her eyes over him checking for injuries.

He shook his head and gave a shaky smile. 'I'm alright … now.'

'Bugs!' Spooky whispered, 'Track, leading off this way.' He was squatting by the open driver's door inspecting the ground and surrounding vegetation. 'It'll be dawn soon, let's get going.'

Hurrying to join Spooky, Bugs called over his shoulder, 'Wait here for the chopper,' as the two of them disappeared into the mountainous scrub.

CHAPTER SEVENTEEN

Above them, Modeen heard the familiar sound of a Sikorsky UH-60 Black Hawk helicopter closing in. As it grew louder, she pulled out her phone, turned it on and held its bright screen toward the sky, waving it in a circular motion. When the trees flexed and shook as the thumping rotors settled into a hover directly above, she turned off the phone and slipped it back into a pocket.

Wolf descended on a rope and landed at her feet, saying gruffly, 'They're lowering a harness for your dad.'

He signalled up to the aircraft and seconds later a harness appeared above their heads. Taking hold of the rope, Modeen held it steady while Wolf strapped her relieved but physically exhausted father into the harness.

'They're taking you to the military base in Townsville, sir.' Wolf had to shout to be heard over the roar of the Black Hawk's rotors. 'They'll check you over and fly you home from there.'

Finding his voice, John Modeen yelled into the blustering downdraft, 'Does my wife know?'

Wolf nodded. 'Yes, sir. Mrs Modeen has been informed that you've been found. Arrangements are being made for her to fly up from Sydney.' He raised a hand and signalled to Ben in the chopper.

As the winch took up the slack in the rope, Modeen gave her father one last quick hug. 'They'll look after you now, Dad.'

Keeping hold of her arm, he frowned as the winch took his weight. 'Aren't you coming?'

'We're not finished yet.' She threw him a reassuring smile as his feet left the ground and he swayed in the air, rising toward the waiting helicopter.

He called, 'Take care, Josephine,' but his words were drowned out by the thump of the four huge blades and the whine of the chopper's twin engines. As he was pulled upward, John Modeen watched his daughter slip on her night vision goggles and follow her big, gruff soldier mate toward the front of the wreck.

Looking upward, he saw a strong arm reaching for him. Ben leaned out and grabbed the harness, pulling him into the safety of the helicopter's cargo hold. Inside, a grimy, weary-looking Sir Robert Woodrow sat strapped to the seat beside an equally exhausted and shell-shocked Michael Johnston. But their eyes lit up and they cheered as Ben guided Modeen onto the bench seat beside them.

Mike yelled, 'John! So glad you're OK,' while Sir Robert leaned forward to slap Modeen on the back.

'Jolly good to see you old man!'

The three men exchanged relieved greetings as Ben retracted and secured the winch. Taking one last look down at the wrecked 4WD, he pulled the door shut and gave the pilot the thumbs-up. The twin engines thundered and the helicopter rose vertically, before banking to speed south-east toward Townsville military base.

'I say.' Sir Robert leaned forward to get Ben's attention. 'I hope this military base of yours has a bar.' At Ben's quizzical glance Sir Robert beamed and stuck both thumbs under his lapels, saying with satisfaction, 'I intend to shout you chaps champers all round.'

Knowing her father was safe gave Modeen a new rush of energy. When she'd scrambled over to stand beside Wolf, he pulled out his phone and turned to her.

'Should we search the wagon first?' His gravelly voice cut through the stillness that had descended on the forest with the chopper's departure.

Modeen examined the terrain around the front of

the vehicle. 'Nah, this thing's not going anywhere. Let's go help Spook and Bugs. I wanna catch this guy.'

With a grunt of agreement, Wolf closed the door on the 4WD and made his way past Modeen to start climbing into the forest below. The sun was rising and threw a helpful glow across their path. They took off their night vision goggles, pulling them down around their necks, and clambered through the thick undergrowth.

'Hang on, Wolf,' a frowning Modeen whispered from behind him. 'How do you know which way they went? You're not even trying to track their route.'

Not bothering to look back, he held his phone above his head, facing it toward her. 'Just followin' the two blue dots,' he drawled.

She bit her lip. 'Of course, I was forgetting Spooky took trackers for them.'

'Yep, the guys are about a kilometre ahead of our current location, which is a long way considering how thick this bush is. Flyin' in on the chopper I saw the lights of a settlement across the valley below us, and reckon that's where everyone's headed.'

She gave a rueful chuckle. 'And here I was thinking your tracking skills had improved leaps and bounds.'

Throwing her a sideways glance, he shook his head. 'You're not going to bring up our trek through East Timor again are you … Mrs Ryan?'

'No.' She laughed aloud. 'If you don't mention the

"Mrs Ryan" thing to anyone, I won't mention how you got us lost in Timor.'

Saying gruffly, 'Deal,' he threw her a wink.

Bumping his solid shoulder with a fist, she added, 'Besides, if Spooky can't track this guy down, nobody can.'

'Yep.' He picked up the pace. 'That boy's part bloodhound that's for sure.'

Following close behind, she noticed he had an M4 carbine slung diagonally across his broad chest. She thumped his shoulder again. 'Hey, how about a trade?'

He stopped and half-turned toward her. 'Whatcha got in mind?'

'Your M4 for this.' She jerked her thumb over her shoulder, indicating the sniper rifle still slung to her back.

'Sure,' he said, his hooded eyes crinkling at the corners, 'I'll take a Barrett over one of these any day.' He handed her the assault rifle and bowed his dark head. 'Take it with my blessing.'

Grateful to trade the heavy rifle for the much lighter M4, she gave an amused snort. 'Lead the way, Mr Ryan. And keep an eye out for taipans, I've heard they like the country up here.'

He gave a deep grunt in reply as he concentrated on finding the best route through the heavy scrub and steep terrain. Some time later, he muttered, 'Wait here,' and scrambled to the top of a rocky outcrop. Squatting, he slung the Barrett from his back and gazed through the sniper rifle's powerful scope, surveying the area below them.

She squinted up at him. 'See anything?'

Slinging the rifle to his back again, he leapt down from the outcrop, landing squarely in front of her. 'River's not far off, and we're closing in on the other two.'

One and a half kilometres later, they reached a gully and followed it along to a sandy clearing on the bank of the Little Mulgrave river. By this time, the sun was over Goldsborough Valley and gaining heat and glaring intensity. As one, they shaded their eyes and reached into their pockets for their NatSec-issued, military-styled sunglasses.

Looking on as Wolf stared at the screen on his phone, she noticed how the glasses enhanced his dark, brooding looks. And when he opened his mouth to speak, his teeth looked white against his deeply tanned skin. Unaware of her scrutiny, he raised a muscular arm and pointed. 'Spooky and Bugs should be just over on the other side of the river, about twenty metres into those trees. We'll cross there,' and he indicated a section of river ahead where the waterway narrowed to about five metres wide.

They made their way to the spot and waded into the river, raising their weapons above their heads as the clear water of the Little Mulgrave crept up to their waists. When they emerged, dripping, on the opposite bank, Bugs and Spooky broke cover from the tree line and waved them over. The four huddled in a small clearing while Spooky gave them a situation report.

'I lost the track on the other side of the river.' With a tilt of his head, he indicated where Wolf and Modeen had emerged from the trees minutes before. 'We've been up and down the bank on both sides.' He narrowed his eyes. 'Whoever this person is, he knows how to cover his tracks. Following him down through the heavy stuff wasn't too difficult, but down here it got a lot tougher.'

Modeen stared at him intently. 'Where do you think he's headed?'

Spooky took out his mobile and brought up a map of the area. Placing his thumb and forefinger on the screen and spreading them apart, he zoomed in on their location, and then paused to wipe beads of sweat from his forehead. 'Goldsborough Valley, I'd reckon, judging by the direction he was travelling.' He gave a sweep of a compact, well-defined arm. 'It's a built-up suburban area over that way. He'll probably try to jack a car there. That's my best guess, anyway.'

Two hundred metres away a pair of dark eyes stared at them through military binoculars, following their movements from his cover on the top of a nearby ridge. Lowering the binoculars, the man pursed his lips and then scowled.

So, Ben's got the team back together … that certainly makes things more interesting.

Keeping his head low, he rose from where he'd been squatting in the dense foliage, slid stealthily down the other side of the ridge, and vanished into the undergrowth.

CHAPTER EIGHTEEN

Spooky clicked off his phone and turned to the others. 'Ben doesn't want us to pursue the fugitive any further. We're to leave the search for the Feds. They're going to send a forensics team to go over the wrecked 4WD for fingerprints, and they plan to set up a road block near Pete's Bridge, where Goldsborough Valley Road meets the Gillies Highway. It's the only way out of the valley by road, so the Feds are thinking they might get lucky.'

The others shared dubious looks as Spooky went on. 'Ben said to tell everyone "Well done". The three hostages are all safe and in good spirits.' He turned to Modeen. 'Your mum's at Lavarack Barracks with your dad.'

Her lips split into a grateful smile and she glanced around the group. 'Thank you guys, for all your help.' She sighed. 'It's been a long day and night.'

'And it's not over yet,' Wolf drawled, gazing up at the towering range behind them. 'We've still gotta climb back up that damn hill.' The others joined him in eyeing the Gillies range, and a couple of them groaned.

Rallying, Bugs gave a toothy grin and said cheerfully, 'Somehow, it doesn't look that bad from here. C'mon, let's get crackin'. Sooner we start, the sooner we get to wash down the dust with a coldie or three.'

By the time they had climbed back to where Modeen had left the old digger's Triumph, a team of two forensic technicians had arrived and was busy dusting the 4WD that Spooky and Bugs had left parked beside the motorbike. One of the technicians was bent over the driver's side door handle, absorbed in checking it for prints.

When Bugs walked up and slapped him on the back, the technician gave a start and whirled around. Finding Bugs standing there in full tactical gear, his eyes widened and he stepped back, bumping against the vehicle. And when Modeen, Wolf and Spooky came to stand behind Bugs, the tech peered anxiously from one to the other. Although tired, they were still menacing figures in their night ops gear and with their weapons slung.

Bugs stepped closer to put an arm around the technician's shoulder and leaned forward to grin into his face. 'Wrong one, mate.' Walking him to the edge of the escarpment, Bugs pointed to the crumpled wreck twenty metres down the slope. '*That's* the one you need to check for prints.' As he gave the disconcerted tech another toothy grin, the other technician came out from where he'd been hiding to join them at the edge.

Behind them, Spooky pulled the remote control from his pocket. The orange indicator lights on the undamaged 4WD flashed as the door locks released.

Hearing that, Bugs gazed down at the crumpled vehicle and then at the technicians standing on either side of him. 'Well,' he said, reaching out to slap them both on a shoulder, 'she's all yours.' He turned and sauntered to the wagon, where Spooky and the others were piling their weapons into the back. As soon as they were all seated, Spooky put the car into gear, took off with a spin of tyres in the gravel, and headed down the range toward Cairns.

As they approached the intersection near Pete's bridge they could see the local police already setting up the road block. Spooky slowed and stopped next to a police officer. Behind the young constable, traffic controllers and road workers were busy setting up black and yellow striped barrier boards and witch's hats.

Rolling down his window, Spooky held up his NatSec ID and enquired, 'Who're you looking for?'

The officer peered at the ID. It didn't mean much to him but looked official enough for him to answer, 'Feds have got us looking for anything unusual or out of the ordinary.' He rested both hands on the 4WD's open window. 'Last time we did this was when a prisoner escaped from Lotus Glen.' As he spoke, he ran his eyes over the others in the vehicle and received a toothy grin from Bugs, a narrow-eyed glance from Wolf, and a smile from Modeen, who tried her best to look innocent.

Dropping his hands and moving away from the car, the officer said, 'Go on through.' About to turn away, he stepped close again and put his hand back on the driver's door. Leaning in, he asked, 'By the way, you haven't seen anyone hooning around on a dark blue Triumph Tiger motorbike, have ya?'

Spooky glanced at Bugs, who shrugged and looked at Wolf and Modeen in the back seat. They were shaking their heads so Spooky turned back to the policeman. 'No, officer. Can't help you, sorry.'

'Thanks anyway.' The officer stepped back from the vehicle and waved them through the road block.

As he accelerated away, Spooky reached up and adjusted the rear view mirror so he could fix Modeen with an intense gaze. After a quick check of the road ahead, he glanced at her and said with a wicked grin, 'That reminds me, nice going with the cop car, Modeen. He could've held things up considerably.'

She remained silent and turned her head to look casually out the side window.

Wolf stared at her, his eyes glinting. 'What did you do?'

She gave a nonchalant shrug of one shoulder. 'It was nothing.' Wanting to change the subject, she leaned forward between Spooky and Bugs. 'Hey, let's book into Citycentre Apartments in Cairns. They're right across the road from the shopping centre. We could grab a bite to eat, buy a change of clothes and a toothbrush, and then crash.'

'Sounds good to me,' Spooky murmured, focusing his attention on the road and the thickening traffic.

The others all nodded in agreement, and Bugs said, 'Me too, 'tho at some stage I'll have to go back up to Rocky Creek and collect my hire car.'

Spooky threw him a sideways glance and shook his head. 'Nah, buddy, Ben's already organised someone to do that. And I threw your duffel in the back when I grabbed the two extra trackers for Wolf to follow.' He jerked a thumb over his shoulder.

Grinning, Bugs bumped his arm with a large fist. 'Onya, Spook, you're a legend.'

———

The following morning, after sleeping soundly most of the previous afternoon and the night, they met for breakfast at Coastal Roast café in the shopping centre. The four of them sat in a booth, Modeen and Wolf on one side, Spooky and Bugs on the other.

Spooky swallowed a mouthful of his hearty 'trucker-style' breakfast and sat back. 'Man this is good, I was starving.' The others were busy eating and didn't answer, so he took another forkful of bacon, egg, toast and grilled tomato and put it to his lips. He opened his mouth but then remembered to say, 'By the way, Ben wants us in a teleconference at o-eight hundred. He'll be calling on my phone, so we can take it in my room.'

Bugs replied, 'Right-o,' and the other two nodded.

Wolf drained his coffee mug and reclined in his seat, casually slinging an arm along the back of the booth he was sharing with Modeen.

At seven fifty-five they were all gathered around a small circular table in Spooky's apartment in Citycentre. His NatSec phone sat in the middle of the table, and at exactly o-eight hundred it vibrated with an incoming call.

Clicking it onto speaker phone, Spooky answered, 'Hey Ben. We're all here.'

'Good.' Ben's deep voice resounded from the speaker. 'I've got Operations Manager Jack Pender on speaker phone. He wants to address us all first up.'

When he came on, Jack's voice was equally deep and his words precise. 'Morning team. I just want to say how proud of you I am, and to pass on the thanks we've received – unofficially of course – from the Australian, US, and British governments, for the safe return of the hostages. Please also accept my personal thanks. It's through your efforts that this mission was a success.' He paused as the four responded with murmurs of 'Thanks', 'Ta', 'Just doin' our job', and 'No worries, Jack,' this last one coming from a beaming Bugs.

'As I told Ben,' Jack went on briskly, 'if this were the army, I would be bestowing medals on every one of you. But as this isn't the army, I've arranged another way to show our gratitude and to celebrate this achievement. You and your partners will be invited to a Prime Ministerial banquet. This is a private, invitation-only function, but the hostages you rescued and other dignitaries will be there, so you'll need to use your aliases. Ben will fill you in on the other details.' He paused again as they expressed their thanks, and then concluded, 'Anyway, that's all from me for now. Again, congratulations team, and well done.'

They heard a chair slide back and footsteps as Jack left the room, and then Ben came on again. 'Yes, well done team.' He wasted no more time getting down to business. 'Luckily for us, MI6, the CIA and the Federal Police haven't kicked up much of a fuss about being left out of our activities. They've been kept busy working with the local constabulary, locking up protestors,' and a hint of amusement crept into his voice, 'along with anyone else within the perimeter of the G20 locations that looks the type to be carrying eggs or anything like a laser pointing device. An extra thousand police officers from all over Australia have been flown in to help, but apart from a few minor skir-mishes, the summit has been progressing without a hitch.'

Ben paused, but when the others remained silent, he continued. 'Now, about the mission mop-up. ASIO has seized all of Akeem Jibril's assets. It appears he had a finance business in Sydney and was channelling a big portion of his investors' funds overseas. We believe he's still out of the country and have arranged for a tag to be placed on his passport. The other insurgents we captured at Rocky Creek turned out to be local thugs. Apart from some tweets about "Islamic suppression" they were relatively small fry.'

When Ben paused again, Modeen spoke up. 'What about the old digger at Rocky Creek? Has his family been informed?'

'Yeah, the intel guys got me some info on him. His name was Ron Frost, "Frosty" to his mates. He never married and his two older brothers were both killed in action in Vietnam. He made it home but was a changed person according to his surviving relatives. They described him as being like a stranger when he came back, a recluse who shunned society.' There was a rustle of papers as Ben went on. 'Veterans Affairs had some recent medical and financial records for him. Looks like Frosty spent his last savings buying that bike and funding a tour around Australia. It was to be his swansong, the poor buggar had the big C and was only given another six months to live. He's going to be given a military funeral, and his head-stone and record will read "KIA, serving his country".'

As Ben's words faded into the stillness, no one spoke. In Spooky's apartment, four heads were bent in respectful silence.

Wolf was the first to speak. 'In my book, dying quick in action beats dying slow in a hospital.' This was greeted with murmurs of agreement. 'So,' he went on, directing his question at the phone and Ben, 'Did forensics come up with any leads from the prints on the wrecked 4WD?'

'No,' Ben answered promptly, 'the Feds and ASIO are still sifting through their databases trying to match the prints, but haven't come up with anything yet.'

'You should get them to try the military database,' Wolf growled. 'I heard the old pom on the chopper say John Modeen was taken by a bloke with an Australian accent. And Spooky reckons the bloke had some training on how to cover his tracks.'

'That's right,' Spooky interjected.

'Noted.' Ben was heard tapping on a keyboard. 'Anything else?' When the others had nothing to add, he said, 'Right then, let's get down to business. Bugs, I want you down here in Melbourne for the next two weeks, we need to get your comms upgraded and I've lined up some training sessions for while you're here.'

Wolf leaned toward Modeen and put his mouth close to her ear. Whispering in his gravelly voice,

'Pierre LeMar,' he drew back and jiggled his dark eyebrows at her.

At their mischievous chuckles, Bugs threw them a puzzled frown as Ben went on. 'The private banquet Jack mentioned is being held next Friday. Wolf, I've talked to your team leader and although he wants you back there in the meantime, he's happy for you to fly across for the function. Now, as we won't be attending as NatSec agents, we'll have to come up with cover stories. Accommodation has been booked for you all at the Grand Hyatt, where the banquet's being held. I'll need numbers to reserve us a table, so let me know if you're bringing someone.'

Spooky's eyes brightened and he piped up, 'Count me in for a plus one.'

The others grinned and Bugs dug him in the ribs, crooning, 'Ooh, you dog!'

'Noted. Now, I want a team meeting with you all at o-eight hundred the Monday after, so you're welcome to stay at the Hyatt for the weekend.' They heard Ben tapping on the keyboard and flicking through some papers on his desk before he spoke again. 'Paul Edwards has informed me of some wreck dives the Navy's doing on the Great Barrier Reef just off Bowen in North Queensland. That's happening the week after the function, so if you're keen to take part just send me an email.' He stopped shuffling papers. 'Right, that's all from me, so if there's nothing else…?' He paused, and when they didn't respond, said with a proud smile in his voice, 'OK, I just want to say again, well done, team.'

'Cheers, Ben,' Spooky and the others chimed.

With a click, he was gone.

'Right.' Modeen sat back in her chair and gazed around the table and her three team mates. 'Where to from here, guys?'

'Looks like I'm in Melbourne for the next two weeks,' Bugs said. 'But first I'll drive up to Port Douglas and drop off Salty's Barrett.' He grinned. 'Think I'll take the black 4WD, I'm quite fond of that beast now.' The others shook their heads at him and chuckled as he went on. 'Then I'll head to Adelaide and spend some time with Cameron.'

Modeen smiled at him. 'How's your son doing?'

'Good, and taller every time I see him. A chip off the old block,' Bugs replied proudly.

'Yeah, well I left my car in Sydney,' Spooky said, 'so I'll fly down there and drive it back to Canberra.'

Modeen looked thoughtful. 'And I'll have to organise a fight to Brisbane and a coach out to Amberley to pick up my car. Then head back to the Gold Coast.'

They all turned to Wolf, who said gruffly, 'As you heard, I'm headin' back home. There are direct flights from Cairns to Perth now, only take around five hours.' He flicked a glance around the table and then his eyes settled on Modeen. 'Guess the next time I see you guys'll be at the banquet.'

CHAPTER NINETEEN

Modeen had just finished dressing in snug-fitting blue jeans and a white polo shirt when her phone buzzed with an incoming text. Running a hand over her damp hair, she flicked open the cover to see a message from Spooky on the screen.

I'm on the 11:55 Sydney flight. You?

She tapped a reply, *12:40 to Brisbane,* and hit send. As she went to put down the phone, it vibrated with another message.

Wanna share a cab to the airport?

She smiled and responded, *See you downstairs in twenty.*

Throwing the last few items in her bag, she left the apartment, locking the door behind her. As she made her way down the corridor, she stopped outside Wolf's door. At her knock, he answered. Behind him the TV was on, set to the news channel. He too was dressed in blue jeans, and a black tee shirt. The shirt clung to his torso and the muscles of his broad chest, and the sleeve bands highlighted his brawny arms. He crossed them, leaned against the door jam, and gazed down at his visitor with a ghost of a smile dancing around his mouth.

Modeen smiled back at him. 'Spook and I are sharing a cab to the airport. What time are you flying out?'

He frowned. 'Not 'til eighteen hundred. Gets me into Perth at twenty-one thirty or thereabouts.'

'Right.' Modeen's smile shook a little at the corners. 'Well then … I guess I'll see you at the banquet next Friday.'

Taking a quick check of the corridor to make sure they were alone, Wolf stepped forward and pulled her close. Leaning down, he whispered, 'Look after yourself, Mrs Ryan,' and brushed her cheek with his lips.

Her voice was thick when she answered, 'You too, Mr Ryan.' Putting a slender hand on his firm chest, she stared into his eyes. 'And thanks, Wolf.'

'Troy.' He smiled into her eyes and, raising a large hand, gently brushed a strand of shiny hair off her forehead.

She nodded and drew back. They stared at each other for a long moment, dark brown eyes gazing intently into thickly-lashed China blue ones, and then she said quietly, 'Seeya … Troy.'

'Seeya, Jo.' He watched as she turned and headed

down the stairs. On the landing she paused and smiled up at him, and then she was gone.

Passing by Bugs' door on the next floor, she stopped and knocked but no one answered. And then Spooky appeared in the doorway opposite. 'Bugs has gone. Said he'd catch up with you next Friday.' Closing the door behind him, Spooky put the key in his pocket. 'Ready to make tracks?'

'Yep, all set.'

They were checking out when their Black and White taxi arrived out the front of the apartment building. They both jumped in the back seat, and the taxi had just pulled away from the kerb when Modeen turned to Spooky and fixed him with an intense, smiling gaze. 'Now, tell me about this plus one of yours.'

Throwing back his head, Spooky laughed. 'I knew it wouldn't take you long!' He sobered but his smile remained. 'Her name's Catalina Hernandez, but I call her "Cat" for short. You'll like her Modeen, she's into kick boxing, martial arts, and keeping fit. That's how we met, actually. She only recently moved to Canberra and joined my gym. I met her about a fortnight ago.'

'Wow, that all happened pretty quickly?'

He shrugged. 'I guess. But it's nothing serious at the moment, we're just dating.'

'So, what does she do, your Catalina?'

'She's a consultant with a recruitment agency in the city, a pretty good one apparently.' He puffed out his chest. 'I told her I'm an insurance salesmen and have to travel a lot.'

'Good cover.' Modeen nodded. 'Catalina Hernandez, hey? Sounds very exotic.'

'Her parents are Hispanic, but she was born in Australia.'

'And have you done a background check on her?'

Spooky looked affronted. 'No! What sort of question is that? Do you do searches on everyone you date?'

'Well....' Modeen looked uncomfortable. 'In our line of work, we have to be careful about who we get close to.' She didn't say any more, and as if by mutual agreement, they changed the subject.

When the taxi pulled up in front of the airport, they paid the driver and got out. Making their way inside the terminal, they collected their tickets from the counter and strolled to the nearest coffee lounge, where they sat at a table toward the back.

After they'd ordered their coffees, Modeen turned to Spooky. 'Bugs must've got away pretty quick after the teleconference with Ben this morning?'

'Yeah, he grabbed the 4WD's keys off me shortly afterward, and said he was going straight up to Port Douglas. He was going to give Ben another call and make arrangements to drop off the vehicle, but was toying with the idea of driving to Melbourne instead of flying.'

'Really?'

Spooky nodded. 'Reckons he likes to drive. He's a bit of a car nut, apparently. Is restoring a Falcon GTHO phase three Shaker that he keeps in mothballs down in Adelaide.'

'That doesn't surprise me.'

The waitress arrived with their coffees. After she left, Modeen took a sip, licked the froth off her lips and said, 'So, is Bugs going to take our weapons down to Melbourne?'

'Yeah, that way Ben can sort them out and arrange for the Amberley gear to go back there.' Spooky threw her a wink. 'Personally, I would've dropped that crap from the highest peak of the Gillies range.'

Modeen snorted. 'It was a bit ordinary, but it did the job.' Resting her chin on her hands, she mused aloud, 'I hope I get my MP5 back, I quite like that rifle.'

The speakers nearby chimed and a nasal voice announced the boarding call for passengers on the flight to Sydney. Finishing their coffees, Modeen and Spooky rose and sauntered over to where the queue was forming outside the departure gate. When he turned to her, she pulled him into a hug and then they bumped fists.

He smiled. 'Seeya next Friday, Modeen.'

'Seeya, Spook. And thanks.' With a final, smiling nod, she turned and headed back to the café.

With forty-five minutes to wait for her flight, she ordered another coffee and sat down at the same table.

Taking out her mobile, she dialled her mother's number.

Freda's voice, when she answered, was warm and excited. 'Oh, Josephine! So glad to hear from you, darling. And how *exciting* about the banquet next week, we can't wait. Never been to a Prime Ministerial function before.'

'Yes Mum. How's Dad doing?'

'Just fine, but I have to tell you … the transformation in your father has been remarkable.'

'Transformation?' Modeen frowned. 'What sort—?'

'In his attitude, love. Since he's been home he's done nothing but brag about you to all our friends … to anyone who'll listen, actually.' She gave a pleased titter, while at the other end of the call, her daughter frowned.

'But is he alright, Mum?'

'Oh yes, love, he's feeling much better now, quite recovered. In fact he's just gone down to the shops to buy a new photo album. You'll never guess what he's planning to do with it.'

'Tell me.'

'He's going to transfer all your old Army photos and newspaper clippings from my scrap book into it. Oh, Josephine, he's so proud of you, and so am I.'

'That's great, Mum, but what's he been saying about me to everyone?'

'Just about how you joined the Army and were accepted into the Special Forces, and how you were involved in his rescue.' Her mother paused, thoughtful. 'That's OK, isn't it love?'

'Well, I'm glad that he's proud of me, but we *are* supposed to try and keep a low profile.' She decided the misunderstanding was to her benefit and kept it going. 'The Army doesn't like everyone knowing who's in the Special Forces.'

'Of course, dear, I'll tell him.'

'And Mum, I'll be seated with the … um … Special Forces people at the banquet, so we'll be trying to stay low key, OK?'

'Don't worry, love, we won't make a fuss.'

————

It was fourteen hundred hours Friday. Modeen stepped into the tenth floor apartment of the Grand Hyatt in Melbourne and dropped her duffel bag onto the plush sofa. She strolled to the window, pulled back the heavy drapes and gazed out at the city. Turning, she went into the lavishly appointed ensuite and washed her face. That felt good. The flight from the Gold Coast had been long and tiring, leaving her feeling lethargic. But at the thought of the function that night, she felt a buzz of excitement.

Going to her bag, she took out the carefully folded, deep burgundy evening gown and hung it in the wardrobe. Taking a step back, she eyed the lustrous folds of heavy silk and the gown's sleek lines. Placing a matching pair of delicately heeled, ankle-strapped sandals beneath the gown, she gave a satisfied nod and decided to take a shower. But before she did, she took out her mobile and sent a quick group text.

In the hotel's expansive foyer below, Wolf strode purposefully through the double glass doors, held open by a liveried doorman. He had his duffel in one hand and a suit pack slung over his shoulder. Dropping his bag on the floor beside the counter, he looked up as the pretty young concierge greeted him warmly.

'Troy Ryan,' he drawled, 'checking in.'

The concierge smiled and nodded, making the gleaming bottle-blonde chignon on the top of her head bob. She pressed a keyboard to wake the blank computer screen and tapped on the keys. 'Very good, Mr Ryan, and welcome to the Melbourne Hyatt. You're in room one o-three on the tenth floor. Mrs Ryan has already arrived.' She handed Wolf a key card, and at his blank look, said, 'I'll need you to sign for the extra key, sir.'

'Hang on.' He gave a puzzled frown. 'You said … Mrs Ryan … has already arrived?'

'Yes sir,' the concierge replied brightly, putting a form in front of him and holding out a pen. 'Your wife checked in about twenty minutes ago.'

'My wife….' Wolf's expression cleared. Slinging his suit pack onto his other shoulder, he took the proffered pen and scrawled a signature on the form.

'I hope you enjoy your stay, sir.'

But her words were lost on Wolf, who had already bent to collect his bag. With a hurried, 'Yeah, thanks,' he turned and strode toward the elevator, a slow smile spreading across his ruggedly handsome features.

Stepping out of the elevator on the tenth floor, he found the room and slid his key card into the slot. The door clicked open and he walked inside.

The room was empty.

Placing his bag next to the duffel already on the sofa, he went into the bedroom.

It too was empty, but there was a scent of green apple shampoo in the air.

Opening the wardrobe door, his lips twitched at the sight of an alluring burgundy gown hanging there. Putting his suit pack beside the gown, he glanced over at the ensuite. The door was partly open and he could see steam billowing around the shower cubicle inside. The shapely female figure standing under the rain shower nozzle turned his way, and he saw her run both hands over her hair and smile shyly at him through the water and steam.

Without further hesitation, he stepped into the ensuite and closed the door.

CHAPTER TWENTY

The Grand Hyatt's RUCO bar was a gleaming showcase of rich mahogany timber and golden floorboards. The subdued glow of the down lights, the soft jazz playing in the background, and the warm tones of the timbers imbued the room with a relaxed and intimate feel. Behind the highly polished bar, three tribal sculptures sat regally atop the counter, making a dramatic statement that was enhanced by the huge mirror backdrop behind them.

Wolf sauntered into the elegant room with Modeen on his arm. They looked around, taking in the room's ambience as they headed to the bar, where Modeen settled herself on a carved timber barstool. Standing beside her, he rested the toe of a polished black shoe on her stool's footrest, and raised a hand to summon the barman.

While waiting for their drinks, he turned to her and

said gruffly but with a twinkle in his dark eyes, 'Tell me, what made you so sure I wouldn't be bringing a plus one to this thing?'

'*Really?*' She threw him a sideways glance, one sweeping eyebrow arched provocatively and an impish grin dancing around her glossed lips.

Wolf was once more rendered speechless by the striking picture she made. Marvelling at what was happening between them, he drank her in, letting his eyes skim over her smooth, side-parted blonde hair tucked neatly behind her ears, and across the lightly made-up features of her strong but feminine face.

His glance slid down to the shimmering burgundy gown he'd admired hanging in the closet earlier, and he caught a tantalising glimpse of creamy cleavage at the gown's lace-edged sweetheart neckline. Against her satiny skin a diamond pendant sparkled at the end of a fine silver chain. He caught his breath when she crossed her long, shapely legs and the skirt's side split parted. Pride at having her by his side welled in his deep chest, and he turned away as their drinks were set in front of him.

Watching him exchange pleasantries with the amiable barman, Modeen admired the cut of Wolf's black Armani tuxedo and the way it hugged his tall, strong physique, thinking what a difference clothes could make to a person. His crisp white shirt contrasted with the tan of his closely-shaven skin and was topped off with the black bow tie she'd helped him fasten earlier, when their proximity had left her with a lingering scent of his manly cologne.

When he turned to hand her a glass of champagne, she smiled into his eyes and received a slow and uncharacteristically intimate smile in return. His normally unruly dark hair was slicked back, revealing his chiselled face. He was a handsome man she decided, taking a sip of the sparkling wine, the crooked set of his nose only added to his rugged charm.

Hearing another couple enter the room, they turned and saw Spooky swaggering toward them, his 'plus one' gripping his arm with a possessive, crimson-tipped hand while the other one rested dramatically at her hip. The dropped-shoulder sleeves of her figure-hugging black gown extended outward from the low neckline, above which the twin mounds of her ample bosom caught the eye of every male in the room. Her long, black hair fell in glossy waves to her waist as she slinked, rather than walked, toward them. Beside her, Spooky strode straight and proud, looking distin-guished in his Dobell tuxedo, white shirt and tradi-tional black tie.

Leaning in to drop a kiss on Modeen's soft cheek, Wolf whispered, 'Does Spooky know we're Mr and Mrs again tonight?'

'Yep,' she murmured, leaning into his embrace, 'I sent a text to let them all know what our cover would be.'

'What about your parents?'

Drawing back, she threw him a significant glance. 'They don't need to know. It's just easier that way.'

Wolf looked at her dubiously as Spooky approached and began making the introductions.

'Jo, Troy, I'd like you to meet Catalina. Cat, these are my good friends, Josephine and Troy Ryan. They're the reason we're here tonight. Josephine's father was one of the hostages who was rescued.'

'Pleased to meet you both.' A waft of rich, musky scent washed over them as Catalina extended a regal, olive-skinned hand to Modeen and then to Wolf.

Hearing her speak, Modeen knew her surprisingly deep voice would sound husky and exotic to men, but to her ears, it had a harsh, almost guttural quality that was in contrast to her petite and polished façade.

Glancing down at the young woman's feet, she took note of the two inch heels on her patent black stilettos. They raised her to Spooky's height, and she assessed Catalina as being a petite five foot six when not in high heels. Watching her face and noticing how her eyes remained shrewd even when her lips were smiling, Modeen mused, *small but tough if I'm any judge of character. And obviously Hispanic with that complexion and those ebony eyes.*

At the sound of a wolf whistle, they all turned to see a well-scrubbed and tuxedoed Bugs striding toward the bar. 'Woohoo,' he grinned, all teeth, 'don't we scrub up well.' Seeing Catalina, his eyes widened and he crooned, 'And who do we have here?' Taking her hand in his, he bent his head and kissed her on the back of the wrist. 'Barry Peterson, ma'am, at your service.'

'Barry, I'd like you to meet Catalina Hernandez,' Spooky said proudly.

'My pleasure, indeed.' He was still holding her hand and she fluttered her heavily made-up eyelashes at him.

Modeen gave an exaggerated pout and grumbled, 'In all the time I've known you, Barry, you've never kissed *my* hand.'

With a bark of laughter, Bugs dropped Catalina's hand and stretched his arms toward Modeen. 'Josephine Ryan, come here.' She slid off her bar stool as he pulled her into a bear hug. 'Know what? I'd forgotten what a beautiful woman you are.' He held her at arm's length and smiled into her eyes.

'Yeah, that's enough,' Wolf growled. 'Hands off my wife.'

With a hasty step back, Bugs raised both hands above his head in a gesture of surrender. He shook his head at Wolf and scowled. 'Know what, man? Marriage has really changed you. You're no fun anymore.'

At the sound of stifled laughter behind him, he turned to the others and said cheerfully, 'Must be my shout, what are we all drinkin'?'

• • •

As a group they moved into the Savoy ballroom and studied the seating chart. Modeen took note of where her father and mother were seated. Their names were listed at another table on the far side of the room, beside Sir Robert and Lady Woodrow, and Michael and Linda Johnston.

'Good to see you all made it.' Ben strode up to stand behind the group.

They turned to greet him with broad smiles and pleased murmurs of, 'Hey, Ben.'

Taking in his statuesque bearing in a tailored tuxedo, Bugs slapped Ben on a broad, suit-coated shoulder and grinned. 'Lookin' sharp there, Mr Smith.'

Modeen glanced around Ben's large frame. 'Where's Emily?'

'Coming, she just had to organise some last-minute things with the babysitter.' Ben glanced over the heads of the others in the room. 'Right, follow me, I know where our table is.' He led the group through the cluster of circular tables and they seated themselves in their assigned places.

Spying the two empty chairs at their table, Spooky asked, 'Who's the eighth person?'

Answering, 'You'll see,' Ben flicked Bugs a half smile, and right on cue, Salty strolled into the ballroom.

Bugs had to take a second look. Salty was shaven, his silver beard neatly trimmed, and he wore a stylish tux. He presented a very different figure from the casually dressed Port Douglas chowder vendor.

'Salty!' Bugs jumped to his feet and took two long strides toward the older man. They shook hands and Bugs clapped him on the shoulder. 'Great to see ya again, old fella!'

'You too, youngster,' Salty chuckled, as Bugs made the introductions to the others at the table. Ben, Spooky and Wolf had all risen and were shaking Salty's hand.

'Some of you have already met my old mate here,' Bugs said, 'and for the benefit of the others, this is Richard Salt.' He threw Salty a wide grin and thumped him on the chest. 'You'd have to look real hard to find a better man, and you *won't* find a better chowder chef anywhere.' Chuckling, Bugs swept an arm to indicate the two women at the table. 'Salty, the lovely ladies here are Josephine and Catalina.' The two women dipped their heads and smiled at the new arrival as he took a seat.

A short time later, Modeen heard Catalina excuse herself and rise from the table. She headed in the direction of the rest rooms, swinging her hips as she walked and looking back to make sure Spooky was watching. Feeling the need to stretch her legs and check her makeup, Modeen rose to follow her, but when she got to the powder room, she saw Catalina hurry past the entrance and right out of the ballroom.

Curious, she followed from a discreet distance and watched Catalina walk to the far corner of the lobby and pull out her phone. Taking a seat at a vacant lounge chair, Catalina rested her elbow on her knee and her chin in her hand, and spoke urgently into the phone, her forehead creased in a forbidding frown the whole time.

Modeen's internal radar twitched as she retraced her steps, deep in thought. In a quiet corner, she pulled her mobile from her purse and scrolled through her contact list. She pressed a button and NatSec resource manager, Leanne Martin, answered promptly.

'Josephine, hi. What can I do for you?'

'I need a background check on a Catalina Hernandez, ASAP. All I know about her is that she's just moved to Canberra and is working as a consultant for a recruitment agency.'

'Right. I'll call you back as soon as I can.'

Switching off her phone, Modeen stopped in at the powder room before returning to the table. There, she found Catalina fawning over Spooky and laughing at something Bugs had said. As Modeen took her seat, a waiter leaned over to fill her crystal flute with champagne from a frosted magnum of Moét, while others weaved between the tables, serving the elegantly presented entrées.

She glanced over at Spooky and enquired innocently, 'How's the insurance business going, Luke?'

His forehead creased for an instant before he said brightly, 'Good. Actually, sales have been on the increase. I should be getting a reasonable bonus at the end of this year judging by the figures.' He was warming to his subject and would have said more had the distinguished-looking master of ceremonies not taken to the podium and called for hush.

'Good evening ladies, gentleman, and distinguished guests. Our prime minister, the honourable Tony Abbott, extends you a warm welcome this evening. We are here to celebrate the safe return of the US Deputy Secretary of State, Michael Johnston, and the British Under-Secretary of State for Foreign and Commonwealth Affairs, Sir Robert Woodrow, along with our own high court magistrate, John Modeen,' and he waved a stately hand toward their table, 'after their recent abduction by a terrorist group known as the Spear of Allah. Of course their safe return would not have been possible without the efforts of our enforcement agencies, assisted by the CIA and MI6. I'd ask you to put your hands together for all involved.'

After the rousing applause, a number of other dignitaries and statesmen gave speeches, after which the main meals were served and the four piece band started to play. When Modeen noticed two empty seats at the end of the table, she leaned toward Wolf and murmured, 'Where's Ben?'

'I saw him pacing outside the ballroom while the speeches were on.'

'What about Emily?'

'She never arrived as far as I can tell.'

Modeen finished her main meal and then rose and made her way through the room and out to the foyer. There she spotted Ben standing, head bent, talking on his phone. She walked toward him, but not wanting to eavesdrop on his conversation, stopped a few metres in front of where he stood. Glancing up, he looked through her at first and then frowned. Raising a hand in a halt gesture, he turned his back to her. A second later he held a hand toward her again, this time spreading his fingers wide and mouthing, 'Five Minutes.'

She nodded and walked back into the ballroom, chewing her bottom lip. Her radar was twitching again.

The main meal dishes had been cleared, and waiters bearing trays of desserts were streaming out of the nearby kitchen. Catching her mother's eye, Modeen threw her a wave on the way back to her table. Taking her seat, she reached under her chair, picked up her purse and checked her phone for messages or missed calls. There were none, so she settled back to listen to Spooky giving an account of how he and Catalina had participated in a car rally in Canberra and finished in third place.

Later, after the dessert dishes had been cleared and everyone was relaxing over tea, coffee or cold drinks, Wolf put his arm around Modeen and leaned close to whisper, 'Did you find out what the story was with Ben?'

She gave a slight shake of her head. 'No, he was busy on the phone.' She frowned. 'He was only going to be five minutes, but that was a while ago—'

She was interrupted by the MC tapping on the microphone and announcing that the meal service had completed for the evening, and that the bar in the ballroom would remain open until midnight. He finished by encouraging the attendees to use the dance floor, mingle and enjoy themselves.

When the band launched into a rousing rendition of Martha and the Muffins' song "Echo Beach", Wolf got to his feet and extended a hand to Modeen. 'Care for a dance, Mrs Ryan?'

She put her slender hand in his, and he lifted her to her feet and led her onto the dance floor, where a handful of people were already twirling and boogying. Once on the floor he turned, drew Modeen forward and then pirouetted her underneath his raised arm. Pulling her close again, they turned in unison, and then he spun her out and then in again in the beginnings of a spritely jive.

Spooky, Catalina and Bugs looked on, the two men with their mouths agape. When Catalina left the table, Bugs turned wide eyes onto Spooky and jerked his head toward Wolf. 'Did you know he could dance?'

'Nope.' Spooky shook his head in disbelief. 'And just look at 'em, will ya? They're burning up the dance floor.'

'I *am* lookin',' Bugs muttered as he stared at the dancers, 'and all I can say is, everyone's got hidden talents, even the Wolf-man.'

When the song ended, a laughing Modeen and Wolf

were leaving the dance floor when they ran into John Modeen, who was on his way to the bar with Sir Robert Woodrow.

John immediately took his daughter's arm, saying, 'Sir Robert, have you met my daughter Josephine?' Wolf went to move away but Sir Robert extended a hand to him, saying, 'Why yes, I do believe we've met. Josephine and her husband were at the Mayoral dinner we attended last month in Brisbane.' He gave Wolf's hand a hearty shake and beamed. 'It's Troy isn't it?'

Wolf could only throw Modeen a rueful glance and say pleasantly, 'That's right, Sir Robert. You have a good memory.' Turning, he saw a stunned John Modeen standing rooted to the spot, staring incredulously at his daughter. To break the uncomfortable silence that had fallen, Wolf clapped John on the shoulder and said amiably, 'Hey, Dad. Got a minute?' Taking Modeen's father to one side, he bent his head to say quietly, 'We're here undercover, sir. We're not really married.'

Behind them, Modeen saw Sir Robert gazing curiously at the two men, so she touched him on the arm and said, 'I'm glad to see you've recovered from your ordeal, Sir Robert.'

'Oh … yes.' He remembered his manners and smiled. 'Thank you, Josephine.'

When the other two men joined them again, Wolf slipped an arm around Modeen's waist and said, 'Now, if you'll excuse us gentlemen?' At their nods, he whisked her away.

As soon as they were out of earshot, Modeen hissed, 'What did you tell dad?'

'That we're here undercover, and not really married. He was a little stunned but I think he understood.' Wolf gazed down at her and shrugged his broad shoulders.

Back at their table, Spooky and Bugs were drinking and chatting, and Catalina was still missing. Taking her phone out of her purse, Modeen found one text message and a missed call from Leanne Martin.

The message read: *Catalina Hernandez is a common name but I found this picture, also a reference to a Catalina Hernandez, daughter of Santiago Batista, Salvatore's elder brother. Catalina & Emilio Hernandez divorced 3 years ago. She still uses his name.*

Modeen clicked on the attachment and a photo of a Hispanic girl filled the screen. Her hair was shorter and she looked about ten years younger, but she had the same ebony eyes, black hair and olive complexion.

It was Spooky's Catalina alright.

CHAPTER TWENTY-ONE

Modeen rose and made her way out to the foyer. It was empty, neither Ben nor Catalina were anywhere to be seen. On an impulse, she went into the powder room and found Catalina leaning on the marble vanity and staring into the mirror as she applied crimson lipstick to her plump, pursed lips.

Looking into the mirror, Modeen found Catalina's dark eyes staring back at her. She held the other woman's gaze and said conversationally, 'Do you prefer Catalina Hernandez … or Catalina Batista?'

Catalina's black eyes narrowed and she gave a wry snort. Still leaning on the vanity, she dropped her chin to her chest and shook her head before straightening and calmly slipping her lipstick into the small silver purse slung across her shoulder. Turning to face Modeen with a stiff smile, she stepped out of her high heels and advanced, her compact but muscular arms raised boxing-style.

Arching one eyebrow, Modeen said incredulously, 'Really? We're going to do this *here* and *now?*' When Catalina kept coming, Modeen flexed her shoulders. 'Alright then.'

Gathering herself for battle, she circled to her left and away from the entry door as Catalina flew at her, throwing a lightning combination of left and right jabs, and then a swift left at her face. As though swatting flies, Modeen deflected the blows easily with the palms of her hands. Six inches taller than her opponent and with a longer reach, she had the advantage.

Jumping forward as though leading with her right leg, Catalina flicked her left foot forward, aiming a kick to Modeen's midsection. Twisting her body full circle to the right, Modeen deflected the kick, while advancing to complete the circle with a sharp blow from her left elbow to the side of Catalina's face.

Sent flying sideways, Catalina crashed hard into the door of one of the cubicles. Momentarily dazed, she shook her head and reached up a finger to wipe a trickle of blood from the corner of her mouth. Seeing the crimson liquid, her lips twisted and she glared at Modeen, eyes blazing. But her expression changed as she rose slowly to her feet, opening her purse as she did so. Facing up to Modeen again, she gave a spiteful leer as her hand whipped out of her purse and she began circling her opponent confidently.

She was holding a small black and silver object. When she pressed a button on its side, a six inch blade flicked out of the handle and glinted under the lights. Thrusting against the cubicle door, she launched herself with a sideways swipe of the blade at Modeen, who jumped backward but felt the tip of the blade nick the fabric of her evening gown and sting against her skin.

Straightening, Catalina lunged again and Modeen caught the wrist of her knife hand in both hers. Catalina immediately stepped in and landed a firm left elbow to Modeen's ribs followed by a right knee to the midsection. Modeen buckled but kept hold of Catalina's wrist to pull her in closer. She jabbed her right elbow under her opponent's chin and Catalina's head snapped backward. Staggering back against the wall, she raised an arm and threw the knife.

Ducking sideways and raising a protective arm over her head, Modeen felt a whisper of air as the knife sailed end for end past her head. It smashed into a side mirror and clattered to the floor. Whirling around to face Catalina, Modeen found herself alone. Racing to the door and out to the foyer, she whipped her head left and right, searching for the other woman, but she was nowhere in sight.

Catalina had gone.

Taking a deep breath, Modeen went back into the powder room to tidy herself before making her way back to the table. With a quick scan of the ballroom, she took her seat next to Wolf.

Spooky glanced over at her, concern in his eyes. 'Have you seen Cat? She's been gone a while.'

'What's up, buddy?' Bugs chuckled, slapping him on the shoulder, 'you worried she's given you the flick?' He tugged at his lapels and puffed out his chest. 'Maybe she's found someone she likes better.'

Modeen didn't speak but pulled out her mobile and opened the message from Leanne. When she placed it on the table in front of Spooky, he threw her a questioning frown and then scrolled through the message.

Bugs leaned in to see the image of a young Catalina on the screen. Taking the phone from Spooky, he read the message and then turned to him, saying solemnly, 'You sure know how to pick'em, mate.'

'Now that I think about it,' Spooky mumbled, 'I reckon she picked me.'

Bugs gave a sympathetic nod. 'Don't feel bad, little buddy, after all she had all the right bait to hook ya. She was female and had a pulse.'

Throwing Bugs a sideways frown, Spooky said sarcastically, 'Nice one. I feel so much better now.'

Wolf had been scrutinising Modeen's flushed face with puzzled concern, but now took the phone from Bugs and studied it for a moment. 'So where is she now?' he drawled.

Modeen looked down at her hands. 'She got away.'

'Oh?' Frowning, Wolf lowered the phone. 'What happened?'

'We were in the ladies and she started throwing punches when I confronted her about this,' and she waved a hand at the phone to indicate Leanne's text message. 'Then she pulled a knife on me and took off.'

'She pulled a *knife* on you?' Spooky said more loudly than he'd intended. Putting his head in his hands and leaning his elbows on the table, he moaned, 'You're right, Bugs, I *do* know how to pick 'em.' Lifting his chin, he snapped his fingers. 'She's got an access key to the apartment.' He sprang to his feet. 'I'll race upstairs and check she's not still there.'

Modeen nodded. 'Worth a try, but I don't think she'd be that stupid.' She took her phone from Wolf. 'I'll give Ben a call in the meantime and see what he wants us to do.'

Ben answered her call almost immediately with a rumbled, 'JD.'

'Where are you?'

There was a short pause and then he said, 'There's been some dramas with the babysitter, and Emily's not feeling well, so I decided to come home.'

Modeen frowned, thinking, *you left without saying anything to us?* Keeping her tone neutral, she said, 'You sound a bit stressed, Ben. Anything I can do?'

He snapped, 'No,' but then went on more calmly. 'Thanks, but I've got some work issues I need to sort out. Anyway, why did you ring?'

'I got Leanne to run a check on Spooky's plus one, and it turns out she's Batista's niece.' She paused but Ben made no comment, so she continued. 'I fronted her about it and she took off.'

Still no response from Ben.

Modeen's voice grew tentative. 'She's got a flat in Canberra, should I get Leanne to send the Feds over there to check it out?'

When he finally answered, Ben's tone sounded flat. 'I'll leave you to handle that, JD, I've got other things I need to focus on.'

Modeen's frown deepened. 'Alright. But don't work too hard, you deserve some rest.'

With a curt, 'See you Monday morning,' Ben ended the call.

Lowering her phone, Modeen pursed her lips and gazed around the table at Wolf, Salty and Bugs. In a quiet voice, she said, 'Something's wrong. Ben left here without telling us, and he sounds really flat and out of sorts. And he didn't seem surprised or even interested when I broke the news about Catalina.'

Salty put down his beer glass and sat forward. 'Don't fret about Ben, little lady. Knowin' him, he's probably got a few jobs on the boil. Besides, everyone's entitled to a bad day, even the boss.'

Wolf put a reassuring hand over hers. 'Salty's probably right. Besides, we'll catch up with Ben on Monday morning.'

Spooky returned to the table a few moments later.

'She wasn't in the apartment.' He flopped into his chair. 'Her small overnight bag is where she left it, and apart from a change of clothes, it's clean.' Holding up a key card, he added, 'I got the hotel to change my access key.'

'Good move.' Modeen filled him in on her phone call to Ben. 'So do you have Catalina's Canberra address so I can give it to the feds?'

'I'll take care of it,' Spooky muttered, sounding dispirited. He picked up his phone and walked to a quiet corner. After a brief conversation, he returned, saying matter-of-factly, 'Done. The feds are on their way there now.'

'Well, I must say I'm a tad disappointed in you young folk,' Salty announced, wagging a gnarled finger at them. 'I thought you'd be partying your hearts out at this shindig, not workin'! This is meant to be a celebration … guess it's up to me to get the cele-bratin' back on track.' He licked his lips. 'My shout! What can I get you all?'

'I'll come up with ya, Salty,' Bugs said, adding as the two of them rose to make their way to the bar, 'You do know there's a tab and the drinks are free?'

'Even better, youngster,' Salty chortled.

Modeen turned to Wolf. 'I'm going over to spend a bit of time with the folks. Come and get me when you're ready to make a move.'

He nodded and watched her make her way across the room to her parents' table.

. . .

At midnight the waiters started clearing the tables as the band leader announced closing time for the Savoy ballroom bar.

Bugs declared, 'Let's have a nightcap at the RUCO bar.'

'Count me in.' Spooky was slouched over the table, looking glum.

With a shake of his dark head Wolf said, 'I'm going to collect the Missus and then we'll probably call it a night.' The others joined him in gazing at Modeen who still sat at the other table, the picture of elegance, laughing and chatting with her parents and the visiting delegates.

'Taking this marriage ruse a bit far, aren't you?' Spooky muttered sourly.

Drawling, 'I dunno,' Wolf got to his feet and threw a smug grin over his shoulder. 'I kinda like it.'

Bugs and Spooky exchanged glances and then watched him saunter over to Modeen's side. When he slipped an arm around her waist, she glanced up at him with a glowing smile.

'Just look at that, will ya?' Spooky muttered enviously and then jerked upright. 'Hey ... you don't think ...?'

Gazing at them, Bugs shook his head in disbelief. 'Well, either they're brilliant actors or they're not pretending.'

Salty chortled and drained his beer glass. Wiping his mouth with the back of a hand, he nodded sagely. 'Like I always say, youngsters, still waters run deep. And good on 'im, I reckon.'

Taking a deep breath, Bugs announced, 'Well,' as he clapped Spooky on a shoulder, 'looks like it's just you, me, and Salty, for that nightcap.'

'Make that the two of you, think I'll turn in.' Salty got stiffly to his feet. 'Now, if ever you're in Port Douglas, young fellas, don't forget to look me up.'

'Thanks, Salty.' Rising, they took turns shaking his hand and then watched him walk out to the foyer. Making their way to the RUCO bar, they ordered their drinks and stood at the bar, leaning on their elbows.

Glancing around the room, Bugs nudged Spooky and tilted his head toward two attractive ladies sitting at a corner booth. 'C'mon, there's no time like the present.' With a wide, toothy grin, Bugs raised his glass and Spooky did the same. Clinking them together, they chimed, 'Who Dares Wins!'

In their apartment, Wolf made his way to the bar fridge. 'Nightcap?'

'Yes please.' Modeen kicked off her shoes and padded over to the window to gaze out at the city lights.

Behind her, Wolf picked up a bottle of shiraz from on top of the bar fridge and perused the label. Satisfied, he took two red wine glasses from the cabinet and quarter-filled them. Carrying the drinks, he joined Modeen at the window and handed her a glass.

She put it to her lips and took a preoccupied sip. Sounding pensive, she murmured, 'You know … I don't know what I would've done if I'd lost my dad.' There were tears in her voice, and she flicked Wolf a watery glance. 'We haven't been close for a long time now, but he's still my dad and I love him.'

Wolf put an arm around her waist and drew her close against his side. 'Everything's alright now. By all accounts, it was pure coincidence that he was taken. He was just in the wrong place at the wrong time.'

She snuggled into his chest and he dropped a kiss on the top of her head. Finishing the last of her wine, she placed the empty glass on the table and closed the curtains. While standing with her back to him, she turned her head and glanced pointedly downward. Seeing that, Wolf set down his glass and unzipped her dress.

As the lustrous folds of burgundy silk slid to the ground revealing her bare, satiny skin, he paced both hands on her shoulders and pressed his lips against her neck. But when he turned her to face him and pulled her close, she flinched and clutched her side. Hastily releasing her, he looked down and saw a blue and purple bruise on the side of her ribs, and a thin blood line just below her naval where the tip of Catalina's blade had nicked the delicate skin.

Raising his eyes to frown into hers, he said gruffly, 'There was a bit more to your encounter with Catalina than you made out.'

She shrugged a bare shoulder and threw him a shy smile. 'Maybe, but I'll be alright.'

'All the same....' Putting both hands on her waist, he bent his head to brush his lips tenderly over the wound, before lifting her in his arms and carrying her into the bedroom.

————

At ten past eight Monday morning, Modeen, Wolf, Spooky and Bugs sat in front of Ben's desk in NatSec HQ.

Modeen glanced at her watch and frowned. 'Ben's never late.' When her phone vibrated with an incoming call, she breathed a sigh of relief. 'This might be him.' But when she pulled her phone out of a pocket and looked at the caller ID, her frown returned. Pressing 'answer' she said, 'Hi Dad, I'm just in a meeting can I call you back?'

'Josephine,' her father said excitedly, 'I've found him.'

Her frown deepened. 'You've found who, Dad?'

'The guy who was driving the car, the one who abducted me.'

She snapped to attention. 'What? Where?'

At her sharp tone, the others glanced at her.

'Here,' her father answered. 'That is, I was transferring your Army photos into the new album and I found him. It's definitely him.'

'But *who* is it Dad?'

'He's in a picture with you and the other guys. You wrote on the back of the photo … "Afghanistan with Ben, Wolf, Spooky, Bugs and Gator".'

At her father's words, she blanched. Sucking in a breath, she closed her eyes and then opened them again, exhaling with a whispered, 'Gator … oh no.'

'I saw the other four with you on Friday night. This guy was the only one missing.'

She didn't speak for a few moments, prompting him to enquire, 'Josephine? You still there?'

'Yeah, Dad, I'm here.' She squeezed her eyes tight, swallowed, and forced herself to speak normally. 'Look, thanks for that. I'd better go, I'll call you after the meeting.' Clicking off the phone, she turned, wide-eyed and pale, toward the others and was about to speak when Ben walked into the room and slumped in his chair, looking haggard. Taking a deep breath, she said, 'Ben, I've just received a call from my father. He's discovered the identity of his kidnapper.' She paused to take another breath. 'Ben … it's Gator. He's alive and here in Australia.'

Eyeing her wearily, Ben turned over a piece of paper that had been facedown on his desk and flicked it toward her with a finger. All four leaned forward to look at it. Seeing 'ASIO Forensic Report' at the top of the page, Modeen glanced questioningly at Ben, who finally spoke.

'That report confirms it. The fingerprints taken from the black 4WD that crashed off the Gillies highway....' Pausing, he ran a hand over his close-cropped hair before saying flatly, '... belong to Eric Crockman.'

The room fell silent.

————

*If you've enjoyed **The Modeen Transformation,** I hope you'll consider submitting a review on your retailer's site and/or on Goodreads, and go on to share Modeen's thrilling adventures in the following nine instalments.*
FHJ

OTHER BOOKS IN THE SERIES

THE MODEEN FACTOR

Introducing kick-butt heroine Jo Modeen
She's beautiful, noble … and deadly

Josephine Dakota Modeen, recipient of the Medal for Gallantry in Action and the first woman to be accepted into the elite SASR, finds life after the Army unfulfilling. When contacted by her old CO, she knows it's not a social call. Ben Logan VC MG doesn't 'do' social calls, at least not to the members of his old squad now living in the 'real' world. Hearing from Ben means a mission, no exceptions….

The books in this series are available in ebook, paperback, and in ebook box sets of three. The first three instalments are also available as audio books from selected retailers.

The 3rd thrilling Modeen instalment

Something's not right about NatSec agent Jo Modeen's latest mission, but how can she question orders from Beta team leader Ben Logan, a man she trusted with her life in the past and wouldn't hesitate to do so again?

She must decide whether to follow her orders, or her instincts....

Realising their activities must be black ops even from NatSec, Modeen's team disperses under deep cover to unravel the web of secrets surrounding the mission, which takes them from country Victoria to Australia's national capital, and across the ocean to Kabul in Afghanistan.

MODEEN CONVERGENCE

The 4th Modeen high-action thriller

For the premier's planned visit to Cairns in far north Queensland, the Feds call on national security agency NatSec to provide assistance with the protection detail. Agent Jo Modeen is assigned the task, what she considers to be a 'babysitting' job ... that is, until an attempt is made on her life and it becomes clear the stakes are higher than first thought.

NatSec Beta Team leader Ben Logan re-forms Modeen's old unit, and they converge on what becomes a complex mission with dangerous links to the past….

MODEEN ROGUE

The 5th Modeen high-octane thriller

Decorated ex-special forces soldier and now national
security agent Josephine Dakota Modeen struggles to
come to terms with the fate of close teammate Troy
'Wolf' Wolverton. Critically injured during the team's
most recent mission, he lies comatose in Brisbane
Hospital's intensive care unit.
And the prognosis for his recovery isn't good.
Driven to pursue the organisation responsible, Modeen
embarks on an unauthorised campaign of retribution.
A campaign that is both personal and perilous.

MODEEN: RULES OF ENGAGEMENT

The 7th thrilling instalment

Modeen and other members of her old squad find themselves defending honour and truth, after being subpoenaed to provide statements to a military inquiry into allegations of war crimes.

Did Ben and his Special Forces squad blatantly breach the ADF's Rules of Engagement while on deployment, or is something more sinister afoot?

MODEEN: FLASHPOINT

The 8th explosive adventure

When an LNG tanker is sunk in the Philippine Sea north of Papua New Guinea, the spotlight falls on the lucrative liquefied natural gas market. Believing an international cartel to be responsible, and that Australia's LNG plants could be at risk, the CIA tasks NatSec with gathering on-site intel.

Modeen's team is deployed to discover the saboteurs' identities, determine their next target, and find out just how far they will go....